HAPPILY Ever After?

MELISSA JOHN

This is a work of fiction. Names, characters, places, and incidents either are the product of the author's imagination or are used fictitiously. Any resemblance to actual persons, living or dead, events, or locales is entirely coincidental.

Copyright © 2023 by Melissa John

All rights reserved. No part of this book may be reproduced or used in any manner without written permission of the copyright owner except for the use of quotations in a book review. For enquiries, please email melissa@melissajohn.co.uk.

First paperback edition November 2023

Book design by Getcovers
Edited by Chloe Cran

ISBN: 9798858651963 (paperback)

www.melissajohn.co.uk

Please Note

This book was written in the UK, where some spelling, grammar and word usage will vary from US English.

Although a closed door, sweet romance, the story includes some sexual and mature topics and language.

Dedicated to

Dreamers

Playlist

Behind the story... BTS – my inspiration. Immerse yourself in the beautiful songs that accompany *Happily Ever After?* Let this playlist transport you to a whimsical world where dreams come true.

Apobangpo. Borahae.

YouTube
youtube.com/@melissajohnauthor
Spotify
bit.ly/SpotifyHEA

So Far Away – Agust D
Lights
Film Out
Home
Spring Day
Sweet Night – V
Hold Me Tight
Jamais-Vu
Crystal Snow
Christmas Tree – V
It's Definitely You – V, Jin
Just One Day
House of Cards
Paradise

Serendipity
Christmas Love – Jimin
Outro: Wings
Fly to My Room
With You – Jimin
Your Eyes Tell
Nothing Like Us – Jungkook
If You – Jungkook
Closer – RM
Lie
Euphoria
Snow Flower – V
Yet to Come
Take Two

CONTENTS

Please Note iii
Dedicated to v
Playlist vii

Part 2: The Secret Diary of Cally Jackson, Aged 40+ 1

July 5
August 9
September... 13
October 17
November 21
December 25
December Part 2!.. 27
Day Before We Leave 29

Part 3: Happily Ever After? 31

Monday: Home 33
Tuesday: Bogoshipda (I Miss You)........................... 45
Tuesday: Plan B 63
Wednesday: Dream Come True 77
Wednesday: O Christmas Tree................................. 97
Wednesday: Mushroom House 113
Thursday: Reality Calls 129
Thursday: Solo 143
Friday: Christmas Magic 157
Friday: Up, Up, and Away 173
Saturday: Slush... 191
Saturday: The Most Wonderful Time of the Year 203
Saturday: Winter Ball 213
Saturday: Saranghae 225

Happily Ever After?	233
Dear Wonderful Reader	241
Acknowledgements	243
Author Bio	245
Reader Bonus	247

PART 2

The Secret Diary of Cally Jackson, Aged 40+

Well, isn't this great? My new costs-an-eye-watering-fortune therapist wants me to write a journal so I can come to terms with having feelings. She says acknowledging that I have feelings is the best way to start the healing process. And apparently, feelings are normal and not a disease. I'm not convinced. As far as I'm concerned, they cause too much pain and need divine intervention to help, because chocolate is not doing the trick.

Maybe I could buy a crystal and forgo all this healing malarkey where *I* have to make all the effort. Why can't I just light some incense and make it all go away?

Now I have to keep a diary – as if I'm aged 11¾ and not on the wrong side of 40. Perhaps I'll treat myself to a sparkly pink journal with a tiny, ineffective lock. And doodle hearts all over it.

So now I have to write in all that imaginary spare time I have with my feet up, drinking cups of tea. Well, *'Ain't nobody got time for that!'* as Lexi says.

One diary entry a month is all the time I can spare.

Although actually, it might help clear my head to write down what's going on, particularly as my life is a shitshow of immense proportions.

So here goes for this month…

July

Dear Diary

Feelings: would not recommend. Zero stars.

They make you cry. Sorry, they make *me* cry. I'm supposed to acknowledge and own my feelings. Considering how much I've spent on two therapy sessions, I would expect to be fixed by now. But apparently that's not how therapy works. And fixed doesn't mean the absence of feelings.

Therapy sucks.

Real life sucks.

Everything is falling apart, including me.

Problem 1: Work

When we got back home, I worked all weekend to get my review edited and polished by Monday morning. I wrote until my fingers bled (not quite true). And all it took was one holiday of a lifetime, one broken marriage, one failed affair, one broken heart, one half-promise of promotion, and a million hours of procrastinating, crying, and having meltdowns. But I did it. And it was a welcome distraction from the hundred loads of laundry we brought back.

So on the first dismal day back at work, I handed it in to the editor. I was so excited when he called me into his office that afternoon. Finally, promotion time. And the all-important payrise I so desperately needed.

But in the life of Cally, nothing ever goes to plan. He wasn't happy. It wasn't what he was looking for. I'd let the magazine down, the resort down, him down, and myself down, blah blah blah.

Before I had thought it through, I told him where he could stick his job. I took back my review and left. I don't care that I tripped on the way out. I said my piece.

Turned out praise from my boss wasn't what my life was lacking after all. It was standing up for myself. Being a badass. And it feels great. Even if I'm now screwed financially and stressed AF.

I have no idea what I'm going to do. Answers on a postcard please, universe. I'm in too much of a panic to think clearly. At this rate, I really am going to let everyone down.

But I have a couple of contacts in publishing, so if I can muster the courage, I'll give them a call.

I'm not sure if this diary thing is working out for me. I feel really miserable now.

But I acknowledged a feeling there – misery. Yay.

Problem 2: Home

We've been back for 43 days, and not only do I have the post-holiday blues, Lexi does too. I keep finding her looking teary while she flicks through our holiday photo book, which she keeps under her pillow. She misses the new friends she made, and the daily fun and excitement. And probably all the attention she got from the lovely staff. I'm sure she would like to escape the hell-hole that is/was home and go back to the peace and tranquillity of living in a fantasy world. Me too.

Nothing compares to living in a fairy tale. As expected, there were no mice sweeping up and no Mrs Hedgehog baking bread when we got home. Nobody puts fresh towels in our bathroom or decorates everywhere with flowers. No champagne on tap. At least I have Barney dog cuddles, but it's back to the humdrum of life in a built-up city, disappointing British summer weather, and trying to decide what to burn for dinner every day. While stressing about *everything*.

Problem 3: Ben

Then, of course, there is the delight of my husband. When Lexi and I returned from our magical summer holiday, I wasted no time in tearing our lives apart by having 'the talk' with Ben.

Which he barely acknowledged. It wasn't that he was upset about losing me or our marriage. It was more anger about losing the perks of having someone to manage his life – keeping him in clean shirts, providing his meals, giving in to his demands.

Ben doesn't want the inconvenience and upheaval of breaking up and refuses to move out. He says if I want to leave, that's fine, but it's his house and he's going nowhere.

I may as well be stuck up in Rapunzel's tower with the choices I have available – I can't afford to find a new home for me and Lexi. I sleep on the couch and have to get up extra early so she doesn't ask questions. I am not coping well with the situation.

Problem 4: Feelings

There are some feelings that are too utterly devastating to even think about. No amount of thinking can heal a heart that's been torn away by circumstance. How do I even begin to recover from an ending that was forced and not from free will?

But Jisung's words get me through each day. That I'm a strong, independent badass. That he wishes I'll come back to him one day.

He is my secret happy place, my comfort, support – like a big hug telling me that I can cope, that I'm going to be OK. That it will all be worth it in the end.

Even if he won't be there to see it.

August

I got my final paycheck. Not quite a pittance, but not enough for Lexi and me to move out. And certainly nowhere near enough to pay for any exclusive resort visits.

I worked out that Lexi would probably be married with her own children by the time I could save enough. Pah! Save! I don't yet have a source of income.

Still, not having to go to work means I can spend more time with Lexi during the school holidays. We've even played princesses (including poor Princess Barney dog) and had afternoon tea.

Bedtimes feel extra special – we snuggle up with fairy-tale books every night, and she reminisces about her experiences at the resort. I try hard to listen and close off my own memories. But our story times have given me an idea to mull over in the very back of my cluttered mind…

Anyway, for now, as soon as Lex is tucked up in bed, I work until the early hours of the morning. Yes, I'm shattered, but yes, I also have an idea of how to make some money:

Cally Jackson, Freelance Writer

I might need to think of a more catchy name… for my new business!!!

Maybe *Cally Jackson, Badass Writer?* Or just *CJ Badass?!*

I plucked up the courage to call my two contacts, and they both agreed I should go freelance. Of course, there are drawbacks, like the lack of a stable monthly income. But if all the stars align etc, there could equally be opportunities. A stable monthly income is great when it's enough, but when it's not, it's time for Super-Badass to step up.

Although, I'm more like Super-Terrified.

But I'm not going to let fear stop me. One way or another, we're going back to Fairy-Tale Wonderland. Oh! That was on the sign in the (awful) maze! And I'm also going to pay rent and stuff too.

Anyhoo, I've been submitting my review for publication in every magazine I can find listed on Google. And I wasn't above being petty enough to send it first of all to my ex-employer's biggest rival.

And then I can write more articles. About things. I can write about any things I like (in accordance with magazine submission criteria – oh how I love small print). Maybe life can start looking up now?

On to more depressing topics, like real life.

Ben still refuses to move out and when he's here, our home is unbearable. Arguments, accusations, blatant disrespect – it's all so wearisome. I'm trying so hard to shield

Lexi from his attitude and behaviour. It breaks my heart to see her starting to withdraw into herself again.

He made a point of staying away for a weekend, without any word, and came back with a love bite. I'm thankful that he often works late and I'm asleep (or pretending to be asleep) (on the couch) when he gets home. I'm sick of the sight of him.

And now for the real nitty gritty of depressing real life.

I'm trying my hardest to hold everything together for Lexi's sake. I save my occasional tears for when I am alone, but the stress is making my hair fall out in clumps and my frown line is getting deeper by the day.

Therapy is not going too well when I can't bring myself to talk about Jisung. I can't open myself to those feelings, acknowledge the heartbreak and hopelessness that haunts me. If I allow those feelings to surface, they will consume me. If I were to question them, reality may slip in and crush the miniscule grain of hope I need to keep me going.

I bought twelve crystals and a pack of incense. Just in case.

I hold on to Jisung's words, and my beautiful bracelet, to get through each day.

September

Lexi's back at school. A relief in many ways that I don't feel 100% responsible for maintaining normality. Her teacher phoned to discuss how withdrawn she has become. I had to come clean with Lex about me and her dad splitting up. She's observant and emotionally intelligent, so she knew things were wrong. Though, she hadn't realised quite how wrong or that there were no repairs possible or wanted. She clung to me in a way I'll sadly never forget.

I don't know how to help her. I don't know how to help myself. I feel useless. I feel alone. There, feelings acknowledged. Now what the hell do I do with them? There are no answers.

Friends? you may ask, dear journal. What friends? How did I get to this grand old age without a single person who wants to be in my company or cares how I am? Am I that awful to be around?

To be fair, it's my own fault. Other people move on with their lives, and old friends drifted away a long time ago. I could never accept any social invitations, never meet for coffee. I could never rely on Ben to be available to *babysit*, and he would never change his plans for me.

I couldn't bring myself to ever phone anyone. Why would anyone want to spend their precious time listening to my woes, always having the same news – nothing new going on in my life. No anecdotes of recent outings, adventures, or anything interesting whatsoever.

And what about *couple friends*? Having friends over for dinner, socialising as a foursome, group gatherings? No such thing. Ben always met his work friends without me. And to be honest, I had always had enough of my colleagues by the end of each day.

I am alone. Lexi is my only friend.

Ben still won't even consider moving out. Lexi and I go out at the weekends when he's home. I can't bear to listen to his ranting while he has to fend for himself by doing his own washing. When he cooks for himself, he demolishes the kitchen and I have to clean for hours before I can use it.

Other than that, not much has changed for him. Except he has more money in his pocket. Finances cause more arguments than ever. He still pays the bills but gives Lexi and me barely anything to live on. Child maintenance is non-existent. He comes and goes, still pays no attention to us or any household chores, and now he gets the whole bed to himself.

But I don't have a single regret about my decision, and his cruel words are having less impact than they once did. Literally the *only* thing I miss about him is having someone to save me from all the massive spiders that keep creeping in and threatening to attack.

Work-wise, I must have been in touch with at least ten million publications by now. I've had the first few replies. But I won't let them discourage me. I'm not giving up. This plan has to work.

In a moment of weakness and desperation, I looked at the photo of Jisung that Lexi took on our first night at Fairy-Tale Wonderland. I zoomed in, and my heart broke all over again. I cried myself to sleep that night. In some ways, it was a relief to finally let it out. In other ways, it cemented my despair.

I know I need to let go and accept we were never meant to be. But how can I move on from a dream I don't want to lose hold of? I feel broken beyond repair, and I can't see a way to fix anything.

I hold on to his words every day. However futile.

October

Autumn arrived, and I held on to my sanity as well as the trees held on to their leaves. Home went from horrific to… equally horrific but in different ways.

My 'husband' brought a woman into my house. It's no longer mine and Lexi's home. We packed our bags the morning we found her standing half naked in our kitchen. I'm almost grateful that it made the decision easy, that it gave me the push I needed to get out of that hellhole. It no longer felt comfortable and wasn't our safe and cosy little space to shut out the world. I had already lost any attachment.

Out of the frying pan we jumped – to Mother's house. Far from ideal, but he's out of my life. I hope I never have to see him again. I feel free! Almost. Free from Rapunzel's tower, but now locked in yet another high tower. The kind of free where I have no choices and have to obey the antiquated rules from my childhood. I'm sure she would still smack me if Lexi wasn't here. She switches from wicked wolf to sweet old grandmother when Lexi walks in the room. I'm still sleeping on a couch.

But Lexi, Barney, and I are together and have a roof over our heads, so I should be grateful. Even though Mother hates dogs. And even with the extra hour round-trip to take Lex to school, and another hour to collect her. So far, Lexi is coping well with the move and leaving her dad. Mother is giving her lots of treats, so it must feel a bit like a holiday for her.

Now for the most exciting news…

My review has been published!

YIPPEEEEEEE!!!!

And not just once, but in 14 publications so far! And I got paid fourteen times!

It was accepted by parenting magazines, luxury holiday magazines, and in an airplane magazine with copies for every seat. By including Lexi's review, although rather unconventional, the article was picked up by family and teen-oriented publications too. Lexi's been chuffed to bits seeing her name in print! I've had some great feedback and made some fantastic connections for future work.

But best of all, it's going to be published in the next edition of the rival's magazine. I win the trophy in the Petty Championships, and it feels so damn good!

And now for even more exciting news!

Spurred on by the smell of success, I started to play with the idea I'd been mulling over in the back of my mind.

I allowed Jisung's encouragement to sink in. I let myself believe once again that I am a badass, and I went for it!

And now I'm a badass writer of children's stories!

Lexi and I took those bedtime fairy tales and asked what if…? Like what if Cinderella was a self-absorbed, selfish liar who used people with a smile painted on her face? That was the first story I wrote.

The ideas and the words have been flowing, and it feels good to use my imagination in a constructive way. My current story is about the lovely three bears who are terrorised by a young woman who breaks into their home. Writing is fun again, not just a way to put food on our table.

Could this badassery be down to the crystals? I bought some more just in case. And a lottery ticket. Mother won't have incense in the house. To be honest, I'm relieved. It stinks.

I still think of his words. I even looked up at the stars one night and imagined he was looking up at the same time. I need to act my age. Or maybe I already am; I've never been this old before. Either way, I'm not ready to let go.

November

Diane sent us a thank-you card! She was thrilled by our review and said we have done her proud. She said they can tell immediately when it is published somewhere because they become inundated with queries and bookings.

What a relief! Our free holiday paid off for them, and I didn't let them down after all. Which got me thinking... Lexi and I proved to be a good investment for the resort... What if we could have an even bigger impact a second time? What if we wrote a review of their *winter wonderland*?

So I wrote back to Diane and pitched my idea. I tried to stay professional and not beg for the chance to return, even though it still felt like begging. And Lexi drew her a pretty picture of the Palace Hotel to add to our plea, I mean, pitch. Diane could be our only hope of going back.

I rush to check the post every morning, but the postal workers keep going on strike, which is driving me insane. So still we wait for a response...

Thankfully, and surprisingly, being a freelance writer is going amazingly well. With its global appeal, my review has attracted a lot of attention, and one assignment is consistently leading to another. Which means income!

But the most incredible news of all… one of my new contacts is a literary agent. We got chatting about the stories I've been writing (taking out my frustrations on all those goody-two-shoes fairy-tale characters to reveal their true colours). Anyway, I sent them to her and she loved them. And she has signed me as a client! Quite possibly THE most exciting thing to happen in my career ever. Next step is for her to find a publisher willing to take a gamble on me…

Life is moving fast, but there is no escaping the bumps in the road that keep knocking me back down.

On Bonfire Night, the ex-husband (not officially, as he still won't agree to a divorce, but it makes me feel better to call him EX) actually took Lexi out to a fireworks display. The first time he's made a proper effort to see his daughter since we left. My poor baby girl was nervous – to see her own father. Mother dealt with him at the door. I didn't need to be reminded of his face.

Meanwhile, I had an anxiety smoke in the garden. But fireworks brought memories flooding back. And I broke down. All the feelings I've been avoiding fell out in one go. Five months' worth of hidden pain that I couldn't acknowledge, hadn't talked to anyone about, hadn't allowed myself to process.

Mother almost called an ambulance. She couldn't help but feel concerned at the hysterical mess she found on the ground.

Despite myself, the whole story spilled. Mother was surprisingly supportive – probably for the first time ever in our turbulent relationship. I think she understood, having coped with my dad for years, and after all the 'uncles' that came and went afterwards.

She didn't even tell me I was stupid for thinking I meant anything to him, or for thinking that he would have given me a second thought once we left, or for desperately wanting to go back to him, or for holding out hope that there was even a remote possibility of ever being happy again.

December

Ho. Bloody. Ho. Merry Miserable Mid-life Crisis-mas. There's been no response from Diane about my pitch to go back. And my agent has received fifteen rejection letters from publishers. I threw the crystals away – they obviously don't work.

Mother announced she was spending Christmas at her friend Beryl's house, so it wasn't worth putting up any decorations, and she didn't want the mess. Wicked witch that she is, this means no opening presents under the tree for Lexi. No fairy lights or garish foil garlands across the ceiling. The one plus side is she won't be making us stand for the national anthem before the King's speech.

Her behaviour brings back too many memories of how thoughtless and neglectful she was as I grew up. I need to get out of her house ASAP, but I'm just not making enough money yet. It's not doing my mental health any good.

Her support that night was a one-off. It's a miracle I grew up to be as well adjusted and sane as I am. How the hell I ended up married to someone just like her, I'll never understand.

So Christmas will just be Lexi, Barney, and me at Mother's house. Christmas Dinner for two and a bone for the dog. And then Lex will be spending a few days with her father at our old house. And I will be alone.

I'm sure this isn't how life is supposed to be. I go through the motions, but I don't really live. I struggle through each day the best I can, drifting, waiting. Waiting for... *something* to take away the pain.

Sometimes I wonder if the longing I feel for Jisung is really just a longing to not be here, in this situation. Except I miss HIM. I miss his smile and those cute dimples. And the way his eyes sparkle. His mischievous grin, his wiggling eyebrows. His calmness, his soothing voice. The softness of his lips on mine. That one kiss to rule them all.

Sometimes I wonder if I imagined it all, if it was just a romantic dream. Except I miss US, and the way we dreamed together, laughed together. I miss how I felt inside when I was with him. How he took hold of my hand, how he held me. And I wear my mushroom house bracelet every day, like a reminder that it was real.

And now I'm crying again.

Maybe the new year will be a new start. Start of what, I have no idea.

Do I still hold on to his words every night? I never stopped.

December Part 2!

Well, Shakira! It's amazing how life can turn around in the split-second of an email pinging into your inbox. I can't believe I'm going to say this, but that email was from Diane!!! I had to read it three times. Then I screamed! (And maybe a little bit of pee came out.)

She was checking we'd received her letter, as she hadn't heard back from us. NO!!! It must be stuck in a backlog somewhere!

She was thrilled by the idea I pitched and has invited Lexi and I for an all-inclusive stay over Christmas in return for writing another review. Screw you, Mr Todgers. I AM going to experience your winter wonderland! I won't be spending Christmas alone in Mother's pokey house. Or eating Christmas Dinner badly cooked by me.

And I can't even bring myself to say who I will see again because it is too exciting for words and I will explode. I've been dancing around the house ever since. Of course, I'm trying to reign in my hopes and expectations, but just the thought of seeing his face again is a dream come true.

I'm so pleased I got rid of the faulty crystals. I shan't risk buying those again.

Lexi is one big smile. I scraped together enough money to take her shopping for thermals and boots, and she's packed her case already – even though we don't leave for another eleven days.

Get this, diary… I even went to the actual hairdressers! No trimming my split ends with nail scissors or dyeing the whole bathroom this time!

Badass Cally is back!

Fairy-Tale Wonderland, here we come!

Day Before We Leave

Who was I trying to kid? My hopes and dreams and expectations are echoing around the whole universe. I'm binge-watching fantasies playing out in my mind like movies – ranging from sweet Hallmark, to romantic running towards each other on the beach (snow plus Gorgeous-Korean-Baywatch-Babe doesn't really mix so well) (or me in a bikini) (or running, for that matter), to full-on your-mother-would-be-ashamed spice.

I am a wreck. A nervous, excited, ecstatic wreck.

It can't be helped.

IT'S A CHRISTMAS MIRACLE!

PART 3

Happily Ever After?

MONDAY

Home

Today is the day I've dreamed of but didn't believe would ever be possible. Today, I will find him waiting for me. I will press my hand to his heart, look into his eyes, and say, *I came back to you. I never forgot you, not for a single moment.* And he will hold me in his arms and tell me I'm home. I will be his, and he will be mine. And we'll live happily ever after.

While I didn't give my lost wedding ring a second thought, I never took off the mushroom house bracelet Jisung gave me. It has been the symbol of hope I have clung to. I couldn't give up on a dream that is everything I want, that has seen me through the misery of these past months. There's no heartache in dreams.

And now, I'm petrified. Six months is a very long time for an over-thinker to run through every possible scenario, every *what if* – past and future. Reliving moments, conversations, considering meanings and motives. Questioning everything.

Today I find out if fantasy can become reality.

***

'Lexi, keep your singing down just a bit,' I speak loudly next to her ear. She claps her hand over her mouth, a flush of pink tinging her cheeks.

'Did you forget you had earphones in?'

She nods, covering her face with her hands.

'Don't worry, I don't think anyone on the bus heard, but you've been getting louder and louder!'

She lets out a whimper from behind her fingers.

'You've got a lovely voice anyway,' I attempt to reassure her.

'Ple-ase can I have some soda, Mum?' She switches to her whiny voice.

'Are you serious?' I turn to face her, eyebrow raised. 'I bet even though Nanny Rose is new, she's *still* heard all about you and your soda vomit shenanigans from last time.'

Lexi giggles, a teasing smile flashing across her face. Her sense of humour is becoming so much like mine – it's truly terrifying.

'Go back to listening to your music, cheeky chops!'

It's strange, going back. I understand why Mrs Life-and-Soul raved about what to expect during our last bus trip to the resort. We know the magic we're about to experience again. We know where to find the hidden treasures. And it's no less exciting. I almost want to turn to the guests sitting behind us to tell them how much they're going to love it.

Nanny Rose calls for our attention. She's dressed the same as Nanny P, a little younger perhaps, and she says the same words but doesn't quite have the same charm and panache.

'Ladies and gentlemen, welcome to Fairy-Tale Wonderland,' Nanny Rose announces (lacking the level of Nanny P's theatrics).

'I hope Nanny P will be there.' Lexi pouts. 'It wouldn't be the same without her.'

I pat her leg beside me. 'I'm sure Nanny Rose is just as nice.' I hope I sounded convincing.

The bus pulls over at the top of the hill and the lights go off. Lexi and I both slowly rise up from our seats, not taking our eyes off the view. The same beautiful, coloured lights, but the landscape… gleaming in the moonlight – a bright, white blanket of snow over the valley. Lexi and I grab each other, both with the widest of open mouths, spluttering gasps and laughs simultaneously. I will *have* to think of another word instead of spectacular – that doesn't begin to describe the scene before us.

'Mum!'

'I know!'

We hug each other tight, still speechless as we fall back into our seats. We knew it was winter, but still… We're used to maybe an inch of snow and then the country comes to a standstill. This is *proper* snow.

'It's beginning to look a lot like Christmas!' Nanny Rose has actually burst into song, and I laugh. And I'm not even cringing, because she's right. We're heading towards Christmas-card-landscape territory. A brand-new experience for Lexi and me.

'We can build giant snowmen and have snowball fights!' Lexi starts bouncing in her seat.

'I'm glad we bought thermals.' Imagine if I'd been stuck in the maze in this weather. I would have frozen to death. I wonder if the hotel shop sells flare guns?

Guests are joining in the bus singalong. Might as well get in the Christmas holiday mood. I join in the occasional lyric I know and *la la la* my way through the rest. Nerves and excitement simmer in the back of my mind as we get closer, but this is a fun distraction. Lexi shields her face as though embarrassed to know me, lowering her hand just to ask, 'What did we do on our first night last time?'

'I can't remember, but I'm sure this time it will all be different anyway.' But I do remember exactly what happened on our first night in summer. When I first saw him. When my life changed. I twiddle with my bracelet. Does he know we're coming today? No! No more thoughts or I'll explode from anticipation. 'Tra lala laaaa, Christmas!' I end on a high note. Lexi squints as though my singing was an off-key screech. As if!

As soon as Nanny Rose begins her final welcome speech, I'm ready. Upon her last words, I grab our coats, take Lexi's hand, and rush towards the front doors. I may have pushed a couple of guests out of the way, but I do have a very good reason – our future lives may depend on it.

I jump off the bus, pulling a hesitant Lexi behind me as she looks around at the unfamiliar, dark surroundings, sticking close to my side. But before anything else, we have to put on our thick, padded coats – it's freezing! Lexi shivers and burrows her face into her scarf as the cold hits. Coats, scarves, gloves, now to run again. We turn towards the big book gate, but it's not there. Nor is there any staff waiting for us. Lexi and I look at each other in confusion before she turns back to Nanny Rose. 'Where are we? Have they dropped us at the wrong place?'

Nanny Rose smiles sweetly, but says nothing. I look up and down the dark road lit by only one street light.

It's not *spooky,* exactly, but Lexi's glove grips my glove. Nanny Rose squeezes through the small crowd of guests towards the trees, and we follow behind.

It's only when we get closer that I see the small door in between the bushes. Double doors, in fact. Old, rustic, wooden wardrobe doors, a handle on each with a key on one side. Ah, I get it. Fairy-Tale Wonderland doesn't need massive neon signs. This is like a hidden winter entrance for the privileged few who get to come here. And we're in on the secret! I love it! It makes me feel special before I've even stepped foot inside.

As we're first in line, Nanny Rose asks Lexi to turn the key. She strains and grunts comically before the stiff lock finally turns. We both pull open one of the doors, which are far heavier than they appear.

A musty smell of woodsmoke fills the air as we walk into the darkness, soft snow crunching under foot. As our eyes try to adjust to the dim lighting, Lexi grabs onto my arm, and tucks herself closely behind my back. We push aside warm, heavy coats that hang in long rows on each side. The sound of muffled laughter and music grows louder, and Lexi looks up at me excitedly as my heart beats faster with each step.

When we reach the other side, bright, twinkling lights illuminate a glistening white reception area, and there we find the friendly faces of all the staff. This time, the hosts are dressed in white, and they welcome us like friends coming to stay for Christmas.

Thalia steps forward to greet us with her beautiful smile, and I pull her into a family hug, thrilled to see our wonderful personal assistant again, until Lexi squeals, runs, and throws herself into the wide-open arms of Nanny P. This in itself is a magical moment – it feels like we're home. There's laughter and excitement, with Lexi giving

Nanny P the longest hug until we're ushered forward for the rest of the busload of guests to come in.

A glass of warmed mulled wine is handed to me, and I turn back to see Lexi licking what looks like a long icicle on a stick. It's the happiest I've seen her probably since we were here last. The happiest I've felt in months too. But I'm keen to get moving.

We're fortunate to be accompanied by Thalia and Nanny P on our walk towards the hotel, and as they guide Lexi and me around the corner, we both stop and gasp. We're in a real-life winter wonderland! Our eyes widen in sheer delight at the glittering snow-covered paradise twinkling with little white lights. The atmosphere is vibrant and thrilling as we weave our way through families of snowmen, each frozen in comical poses. Lexi's infectious laughter echoes in the crisp winter night as she pauses to admire the playful scenes and surprises at every twist and turn.

Fairy-Tale Wonderland isn't made for rushing through. There's too much to see, so many tiny, extraordinary details that aren't to be missed. And Lexi doesn't want to miss a single thing.

It's a festive feast for the senses with the tinkle of distant sleigh bells, frosty chill freezing our noses, and aromas of pine trees and, well, Christmas.

I can already feel the weight of real life lifting from my shoulders, and each icy breath brings a sense of exhilaration mingled with serenity. Even now, my heart has grown three sizes at Lexi's giggles as she skips through the snow. This place is like no other — a sanctuary from the ordinary, and I want to savour every magical second.

But I'm torn between awe and impatience. As we head to the hotel, each snowy step is beginning to feel like a slog. Yes, it's pretty and sparkly, and a world away from being at Mother's in the city, but I've waited so long to see him.

Lexi is deep in conversation about school with Nanny P, while poor Thalia is trying to chat with me. But I can't get out of my head; my thoughts are spinning.

We make our way through the tree tunnel of lights, emerging into the village square to the harmonies of carol singers filling the air with festive cheer. The sights and atmosphere that greets us is nothing short of breathtaking.

The Palace Hotel, emanating its purple glow and with its majestic snow-topped towers, stands proud as a symbol of hopes and dreams. Below, a fountain of unicorns frozen in place, captures our attention with its vibrant lights, and the big magical tree of dreams or wishes, whichever it was, is illuminated with icicle lights, casting a captivating glow all around. It's a familiar sight, but somehow, looks even more magical than in the summer.

Lexi tugs on my arm, 'Mum, it's so beautiful.' Her voice is filled with wonder, excitement bubbling beneath as though she may burst any second. 'Oh, Mum! Look at the fairies!' She bounces on her toes ready to pull me towards the huddle of fairies dressed in magnificent white costumes, each with different-coloured iridescent wings.

Distracted by the delicious aroma of roasting chestnuts from nearby stands, Lexi's stomach growls. 'Mmm! They smell so good. Can we get some?' She pulls my hand, snapping me out of this winter wonderland dream that we are so lucky we get to experience.

'Your bus arrived a little later than we were expecting.' Thalia brings us both back to the present, checking her watch and tapping on its screen. 'The evening show is about to begin. I'm sure you won't want to miss it. Shall we go straight there?'

'Oh. Sure.' I try to hide the disappointment in my voice. My heart sinks as I follow along dutifully. After all this waiting, now I have to sit through some show first before I can finally lay eyes on him? It's pure torture being so close, yet having to hold off on the moment I've been dreaming of for months.

I shiver against the cold, but it's nothing compared to the icy grip of apprehension inside me. What if he's forgotten me? No, he wouldn't break his promise. I just need to hold on a little longer before I can learn if fairy tales do come true.

'It's not outside in the cold, is it?' I can't imagine sitting out here for long before we turn to ice statues – much like my heart has been all this time without him. *Just get through this, Cally. The waiting will make seeing his smile again all the sweeter.*

'It will be lovely and warm,' Thalia reassures us with a big smile.

Lexi's disappointed little face looks up to Nanny P, her longing to explore the enchanting world around her palpable. 'No time to meet the fairies?'

'Not just yet, sweetheart.' Nanny P gently twists one of Lexi's plaits around her finger.

Lexi pouts. 'But...'

'But you're going to love the show.' The mischievous twinkle in Nanny P's eyes seems to do the trick at bringing a smile back to Lexi's face.

Thalia leads us with eager steps around the palace to the Stage Garden. Lexi runs on ahead, keen to discover the wonders that await.

***

As we approach, the sight of a grand yurt before us leaves us momentarily speechless, its size and vibrant colours commanding attention. When we step inside, friendly cloakroom attendant fairies with sparkling wings gracefully collect our boots, coats, and gloves. With a flourish, they present us each with cosy slippers and a plush blanket. Lexi and I exchange delighted glances, unable to contain our giggles at this whimsical, new experience that feels like a secret shared between friends.

We step through a curtain into the main yurt area, where a stage beckons at the far end, rows of seats arranged neatly before it. Crackling fire pits are scattered throughout, creating a cosy ambiance. As we take our seats and snuggle under our blankets, a smiley fairy glides towards us, carrying two steaming mugs of hot chocolate. Lexi wastes no time in diving into the swirls of cream piled high on top, her face covered in chocolate sprinkles. I wrap my hands around my mug, feeling the gentle heat seep into my palms, smiling at the mini gingerbread man perched on the side. Oh how I've missed these wonderful treats. I wonder if *wonderful* will be my word of the week.

We settle back just as the lights dim. A hush falls over the crowd, and a tingling sensation of anticipation fills the air. A spotlight appears centre stage, and then Todgers appears. He walks to the microphone in the middle – without his usual swagger. He's dressed with the same flair and exudes the same charm as he gives his welcome speech, but he looks frail and has aged considerably. I wonder if he's sick?

I also wonder if maybe this is when I will lay eyes on Prince Charming at long last? I take a deep breath, attempting to steady my racing heart, but tremors pulse through my body. Time seems to stand still as the music begins, my eyes laser-focused on the stage, searching for any sign of his presence. The show starts and I'm pretty sure I stop breathing all together. Lexi is riveted by the Nutcracker performance. Her eyes shine at the superb ballet dancers twirling across the stage in their fantastical costumes. I can practically see the inspiration seeping into her, igniting dreams of being on that very stage. But guilt clenches my heart like a vice. She has been so keen to start dance lessons since we were here in the summer, before her home life was torn apart. It breaks me knowing that I've let her down, that I'm failing as a mother.

Loud music and flashing lights bring my attention back to the stage and I watch, fixated, waiting.

When the show comes to an end, there's no special appearance from Prince Charming, and I begin to breathe again. Heavy, disappointed breaths.

Lexi is first to jump up and lead the audience's standing ovation. I fake smile through the applause and throughout the hassle of boot collection, even though when they hand back our outdoor gear, our boots have been cleaned and our coats and gloves are warm and dry. Arrangements are made for Lexi to go and explore with Nanny P while I go to reception to get our room keys.

I trudge to the hotel as fast as my emerging new-boot blisters allow, my heart pounding wildly. This is the moment I've been longing for – when I will finally see his face again. Nerves churn within me. What if too much has changed? But, with far more confidence wearing leggings minus vomit stains, I enter the palace – and stop still – looking around in total awe, my breath catching in my throat. The hotel has undergone an awe-inspiring transformation into the opulent home of Christmas spirit itself. With enough twinkling lights that can surely be seen from space, the glitz and glamour is fabulously over the top, yet still looks elegant and sophisticated.

My gaze rises, drawn to the centrepiece that steals the spotlight – a colossal, gravity-defying, upside-down Christmas tree suspended mid-air. Adorned with a cascade of diamonds, its shimmering hues reflect a kaleidoscope of colours throughout the grand lobby.

As I tear my eyes away from the mesmerizing heights, I am drawn to the floor level, where a sprawling miniature Christmas village unfolds like a scene from a fairy-tale. Tiny houses with twinkling lights and wreaths line the cobblestone streets, their windows glowing with warmth and merriment. A miniature ice rink sparkles with frost-kissed magic, inviting mini skaters to twirl and glide upon its icy surface. The air is infused with the scent of pine, mingling with the sense of Christmas joy that fills every corner of this magnificent display.

This is no ordinary lobby – it is a gateway to wonder and enchantment. Every detail, every shimmering light and carefully crafted ornament tells a story of Christmas splendour. It is a place where dreams and reality intertwine, where the spirit of Christmas dances on every surface, and where the child in me can't help but believe in the magic that surrounds us.

How does the resort do this to me? It's ridiculous! Within seconds, it's turned me from a fully grown, worn-down adult into a cheesy-smiling kid waiting for Santa! But, in my defence, it is truly spectacular.

The magic fades in an instant, and I frantically scan the lobby, my eyes darting from face to face. I crane my neck, searching for any glimpse of his charming smile among the sea of unfamiliar faces. My heartbeat echoes in my ears. Could he be here? He has to be here. But instead of Jisung, I turn to see Diane, her arms outstretched and a bright smile on her face, ready to draw me into a hug.

'Cally, my dear, you're here!'

I pull back from her grip, returning her smile. 'It's lovely to see you. How are you?'

'Very well.' She smiles, but her pale face and the dark rings around her eyes, visible despite her make-up, betray her words. 'How was your journey?'

'All went smoothly. How's Mr Todgers?' I ask cautiously, not wanting to intrude on her personal matters.

'Fine for now. We'll talk more in the morning. You go and unpack and relax for the evening. You've had a long trip.'

I put my hand on her arm and give her a squeeze. I'm concerned for my friend; she looks so tired and stressed.

'Has Cinderella been helping you out at all?'

'You mean Taylor? Oh, well, she moved on to, err… bigger and better things.'

Eyes wide, my throat constricts and I force out the question. 'And Prince Charming?'

'He's not here.'

The shock of her words sends a jolt through my body. The last thing I remember is stumbling backwards.

TUESDAY

Bogoshipda
(I Miss You)

I'm not sure if I slept or was trapped in a waking nightmare. I must have fainted or gone into shock, or both, last night. I have a vague recollection of people standing over me, and I remember saying I didn't need an ambulance. Thankfully Thalia and Nanny P were on hand to help us to our room.

Now I have to face the day, paint a smile on my face, be full of fun and Christmas cheer for Lexi, focus on my work assignment for Diane, and find out what the hell is going on. I have to hold myself together, for Lexi's sake.

'Mum, are you awake?'

'Hmmm, are you?'

'Erm, yeah. Have you still got a headache?'

'I'm fine now, thank you.' I guess that must have been the excuse I used for last night's blackout 'incident'.

'Shouldn't you get up?'

All I want to do is stay hidden under my duvet, especially as it's a luxury to stretch out in a bed rather than be cramped on a couch. Still, I've become an expert at pretending all is well and carrying on despite my life falling apart. Here goes…

I force myself to leap out of bed, singing 'Good morning!' in a voice that sounds way too cheerful – Lexi's bound to realise something's wrong.

She's already up and dressed, sitting under a sparkling white Christmas tree surrounded by bows and ribbons and glossy paper, unwrapping all the presents beneath. It's not Christmas morning, but I don't want to start our holiday by telling her off. I can't dampen her spirits with my own darkness. I take a deep breath and push aside my inner turmoil, determined to create a magical holiday experience for her. 'Ooh Lex, what have you got there?'

'I got bored waiting for you. Aren't you mad?'

'Mad you got presents? Of course not!' I chirp. 'Who are they from?'

'From Fairy-Tale Wonderland. I think we got these instead of the baskets we had before.'

'Ah, how lovely. Have fun. I'm just jumping in the shower quickly.'

Twenty minutes later, I'm dressed in an itchy snowman jumper, trying out all the freebie toiletries, and applying make-up. Painting on that smile in a glossy pink. Lexi reels off a list of all the gifts we've been spoilt with: a reindeer teddy, sunglasses (don't they realise it's winter?), lip balm, mini gingerbread men, and gorgeous Christmas tree baubles with our names on.

I finally take a proper look around our room; it's even more gorgeous than our previous room. I wonder if we've been upgraded? It is the epitome of Christmas magic – chic, luxurious, white with delicate touches of pale pink and the soft glow of twinkling lights. It feels like a sanctuary, shielding me from real life, even if it's just for a short while.

Lexi is nestled under a furry throw in a snuggly nook by the corner windows, her new plush reindeer in her lap. Her bed is set back into the wall again with sparkling pink curtains, and my bed has the softest, cuddliest pink throw and cushions. I'm sitting at the dressing table lit with candelabras, my feet burrowing into a white, furry rug. Even the bathroom sink is pink and heart-shaped.

I could live here forever. But right now, I need coffee.

Lexi and I head to one of the small dining areas, admiring all the Christmas trees along the way. Trees of all sizes and colours, each uniquely decorated – a pink, fluffy-feathered tree; fairy-tale-themed trees; a tall tree dressed as a snowman; and a huge tree covered with hanging chocolate truffles. We take a couple each as we pass – I bet they have to be replenished all day long.

Everywhere we look is Christmas. More Christmas than we could ever dream of. It's so Christmas that it almost takes my mind off needing to know exactly where I can find Jisung.

Lexi and I both hurry down a bowl of cinnamon-spiced porridge with figs and berries, smothered in honey. Lex enjoys a warm gingerbread smoothie – which sounds disgusting, but she swears it's delicious. I try a creamy whipped coffee – which is now my favourite thing in the entire world.

Once we've bundled Lexi up in her cold-weather gear, we trundle out for the morning's activities.

The cheerful voice of one of the leaders in their vibrant orange snowsuits sings out, inviting Lexi to join the festivities. 'Welcome! Come and get a name tag and pick a team – robins or bluebirds!'

The excitement buzzes around us as children gather at tables covered in colourful name tags.

'See you later, Mum.' Lexi runs off to collect a blue bib and joins her lively bluebird teammates.

'Have fun, Lex!' I call after her, and without a moment's hesitation, I return inside to the blissful warmth of the hotel.

***

Diane is standing in her office doorway, ready to greet me as I approach.

'Good morning. Come in, come in.' She puts her arm around my shoulders and guides me inside. 'Did you sleep well, dear?'

'Yes, thank you,' I lie. 'Our room is wonderful. Thank you so much.'

'You're very welcome. Coffee? Or should I get you some breakfast tea?'

'Coffee's perfect, thank you.'

Diane looks her usual elegant and professional self. Wearing proper shoes. I glance down at my complimentary slippers. I hope she remembers I don't do dressing up.

I wince as I take a seat on her shiny new couch and pray to the coffee gods that I don't spill a drop and ruin this one. Diane hands me a mug and sits facing me. She still has tired eyes, but sounds chirpy.

'How are you this morning? You must have been exhausted last night.'

'Just a bad headache, but I'm fine now.' By fine, I mean feeling like I've been hit by a snowplough.

'That's good. And how has life been treating you since we saw you last?'

'Um, it's been eventful.' My shoulders sink, and I let out an accidental sigh. Diane nods at me to elaborate. She has such a kind face, I feel comfortable telling her the truth.

'The short version is… I'm divorcing my husband, and me and Lexi are homeless, staying with my mother temporarily.' I loosen my grip on my mug before it crushes in my hands.

Diane nods again as though not entirely surprised. 'I'm sorry to hear that.'

'The good news is that my freelance writing business is starting to take off, and at last, I'm following my dreams of writing children's books.' At least I have something cheery to tell her so I don't seem as doom and gloom as I feel inside. She smiles, and her eyes brighten.

'Oh yes, I can see you writing stories for little ones. I'm sure they are adorable.'

'I hope so.' I give a shy smile after my imaginary clever-girl pat on the head. 'I just have to hope I can find a publisher who thinks so too.' I wave my hand, leaning forward towards Diane; I need to stop speaking before I over-share or the gloom sneaks in again. 'But enough about me. How have you been?'

'Things have settled for now.' Diane takes a deep breath through her nose, making her nostrils flare. 'After Frank had a second heart attack, there were complications. He's under strict instructions to take it easy.'

My hand flies to my chest. 'Oh my goodness, I'm so sorry. Is he all right?'

Diane nods as she takes a sip of coffee. 'He's out of hospital and doing well.' She manages a weak smile and pauses to regain her composure. 'He's stepped down from most of his duties here. But he's not one for change, and hasn't taken too well to some of the resort improvements.' She pauses again as though the magnitude of all she's been through is just hitting her.

'And how have you been?' I lean in towards her, rubbing my forehead, which is beginning to hurt from my eyebrows being so scrunched with concern.

'It's been a little challenging.'

She hides her sigh well. I want to give her a cuddle. No wonder she looks tired; she must be under tremendous strain.

After a few moments, she sits up straight and her demeanour strengthens.

'But a new investor came on board and we had a few staff changes. Now I have a new assistant; you'll meet Shana later.'

I can tell from Diane's smile that it's a huge relief to have some help. I can't imagine how stressful it is to manage this resort alone, even without your husband becoming ill.

'It must have been very hard for both of you.' I pass her the plate of biscuits. Not the grandest of sympathy gestures, but I don't know what I can do.

'Was Taylor one of the difficult changes? It couldn't have been easy with Frank's niece moving away.'

'Yes, sadly. I shouldn't really say, but we had so many complaints about her behaviour from the other staff, I had no option but to let her go.'

'Oh dear.' I can't even make it sound like I'm surprised by the news.

Holding my breath, with the deepest sense of dread, I have to ask the most difficult question. 'And Jisung?'

'Oh yes, the two of you were friends.'

'No. Well, yes.' Oh god, please don't say he was fired because of me. We didn't break the no-staff-relationships rule, did we? 'I just wanted to check if he got his replacement coat.'

'He'll be back at lunchtime. He's had some important meetings to attend.'

I let out the loudest breath and fall back against the couch. Thankfully spilling only a small amount of coffee… on myself.

I stand up to shake off my trousers, breathing hard. My knees shake, and I sit down, drink coffee, take off my jumper, smooth my hair, try to breathe normally. Not an over-reaction about a coat at all. Thank you, coat gods, for this miracle. I owe you one.

'Do you need a break, dear? Are you getting a headache again?'

'No, no, I'm fine, sorry.' A half truth. Half ridiculously excited, half nervous mess. Three hours until midday. I'm buzzing as if I've had ten pots of coffee, and I want to jump up and down on the couch like Lexi would. I take a deep breath, unable to hide the change in my whole energy. 'Let's talk work. What can I do to help you?'

Diane opens her office door and calls for Shana to join us.

Shana is blessed with lustrous, dark hair in a ponytail down to her waist. The sleek, straight hair of every curly-haired girl's dreams, I'm sure. I imagine being able to run my fingers through without any knots. I quickly bring my focus back to the room and stand up to shake her hand while Diane makes the introductions.

'Shana, my life-saving assistant. Cally, our esteemed VIP guest and extraordinarily talented writer.'

My cheeks warm. Diane has extremely high expectations.

'Do take a seat. Now Shana, could you kindly bring Cally up to speed on our plans?'

I quickly take out my notepad and pen. Work mode switched on.

'Due to the sudden increase in bookings' – Shana pauses and gives me a nod as if the increase is all due to my article – 'and the knock-on effect of the other article and subsequent legal issues, we want to focus on...'

'Other article?' What have I missed? 'Legal issues?' What am I up against here? I look to each of them to fill me in.

Shana's eyes widen, staring at Diane. 'We want to focus on...' she repeats slowly, her voice getting quieter. Her eyes almost pop out of her head as she waits for Diane's reaction.

Diane lets out a long sigh through her nose, her lips pinched as though squeezing back her annoyance. I hope she's not annoyed at me for being nosy. 'Sorry, you don't have to tell me. I'm not here as a journalist.'

'No, no, it's fine, dear. As you know, the other journalist here in the summer didn't leave us on the best of terms.'

She must mean that evil Miss Suit. My anger levels rise even before I hear what she's been up to.

'The article she published about us was, hmm, scathing.' What? How did I not know about this?

Diane crosses her legs, clasping her hands around her knee so tightly that her knuckles are white. 'We are currently taking legal action.'

'Oh Diane, that's awful.' My heart aches for her. 'It must be so hard on you and Mr Todgers.'

She takes in a sharp breath. 'It's put a strain on things, on Frank especially... and it has had a negative effect on our bookings.' She glances away as her voice trails off. I can see it's too difficult for her to continue.

I'm inwardly raging at the effect that nasty woman has had on Diane, but I take a second to consider that letting out my anger won't help. Diane's been through enough, and she doesn't need me exacerbating the situation. But... no way am I going to let Miss Suit get one up on us after the trouble she tried to cause for Jisung.

Save-the-day Super-Cally jumps in before I can keep my mouth shut. 'Well, I'm here now. I'm the resort's biggest fan, and I shall write the most glowing review ever and have it featured in the largest publications worldwide. Any damage that woman has done will pale into insignificance. Just leave it with me.'

Diane's face lights up, and the energy of the room rises to meet my enthusiasm. Diane and I pause to drink our coffee, and now that Shana's eyes have returned to normal, she continues speaking. 'We want to focus on...'

I can't concentrate on what they want to focus on. What the hell have I done? How did I just shoulder responsibility for the resort's success? *Volunteer* to shoulder responsibility. *Keep smiling; panic later.*

'What do you think, Cally?'

I focus back on Diane. I don't think anything; I wasn't listening. Her tone and expression suggests eager anticipation.

'It sounds great.' I smile and look excited. Their faces suggest that was the correct response.

'We're looking to refine our product development to provide a first-class service to our guests,' Shana adds. I can't cope with business speak right now. Her words wash over me, blending into a blur of business jargon.

'We hoped you might note any further improvements we could make to meet customer expectations.' What did she say?

Diane turns in my direction, uncrosses her legs, and leans towards me. 'How does that sound? It would be a huge favour to me.'

'No problem. I'll get right on it.' My head is in a spin. I need air. Now what have I just agreed to?

I slap my thighs, about to stand, and Diane puts her hand on my knee to stay put. She nods, and Shana understands this to mean she can leave.

'You'll need some time to think and work your magic. I suggest you go over to the spa for a relaxing massage to get the ideas flowing.'

I swap work panic for Jisung panic and glance up at the clock. 'But I–'

'It's all booked for you, dear. You'll be back by lunchtime.'

The kindness in her face makes me take a calming breath. 'This is very unexpected, thank you.' I give her a hug. Screw professionalism. She's Aunty Diane.

***

Ahhh, the spa. A gentle wave of soothing lavender and eucalyptus envelops me as I enter. The smell of calm. A polite, white-uniformed young woman greets me by name, her voice as soft as a whisper, and guides me towards a secluded treatment room.

'Abbi!'

'Cally! I saw your name on the booking; I wondered if it might be you.' We both lean in for *lovely to see you* hugs, then straight away she passes me a glass of champagne.

I shake my head. 'I shouldn't; I'm working.'

'No working allowed in here! Treatment rooms are for total relaxation.' I love her mischievous grin; it really is great to see her again.

'Oh, go on then. You've twisted my arm.' I take a sip of champagne. It's 9.45 am. Oh well, it might help the two-and-a-quarter hours to pass more quickly.

'How are you doing?' she asks while preparing the massage oils.

'Very good.' Polite lie. 'How are things with you? Any juicy gossip?'

'Literally living the dream!'

There's that mischievous grin again. I start to undress behind the screen, as instructed by a point of her hand.

'I have a man!' Abbi blurts out in a sing-song voice.

I pop my head back out again, eyebrow raised. 'Oooh, spill!'

Abbi's cheeks flush pink as she arranges the towels. 'Well, nearly. It's not official, so I can't say too much, too soon.' She glances up, eyes sparkling. 'But I can say tall, dark, and handsome...'

'Abbi's got a boyfriend!' I tease, as I settle onto the soft, heated bed and cover myself with the warm, fluffy towels.

'Shush!' She swats my arm with a giggle and dims the lighting to create just the right ambience with aromatherapy candles and soft music.

'Now, it's time for you to relax.'

I let out a groan on her first strokes of my back. It's the first time my skin has been touched for... so long, I can't even remember.

***

As much as I had planned to think about words, the peaceful atmosphere lulled me into relaxation. A massage was precisely what my mind and body needed, but my soul remained on clock-watch until the very end.

'Thank you so much, Abbi. You have magic hands. That was incredible.'

'You had lots of knots and tight muscles. Everything all right?'

She doesn't need to hear I'm just having my usual breakdown over every part of my life. 'I expect it's just the divorce.'

She places her hand on my shoulder. 'Oh Cally, I'm so sorry.'

I'm surprised by how good it feels to be comforted, having mainly dealt with the situation alone. 'Thank you. The ex has been a nightmare.' I sigh.

'We must meet for a drink so you can share the load.' She gives me a hug, and I respond with a huge smile.

'That would be great.' Ohmygosh! A social invitation! It's been even longer since I've had one of those. 'I suppose I better go and do some work now!'

'Wrap up warm. We don't want you catching the sniffles that have been going around.' Abbi gives my hand a squeeze as I leave her treatment room. How I've missed having a friend.

***

Outdoors feels extra cold after the lovely warmth of oils and hands and heated duvets. But the air is still and refreshing. I have an hour to kill. Enough time for a walk around the Secret Garden.

The golden mirror is still at the hidden entrance. I run my gloved fingers over the glass, clearing the fresh layer of snow covering its message: *Find strength in solitude.* Following the path inside, the serene, snow-covered landscape of the Secret Garden glistens, inviting me to embrace its tranquillity.

Its message resonates now more than ever before – especially with memories of a toxic marriage still too fresh in my mind. Although life was already pretty solitary when I lived with Ben, I do feel stronger without the weight of his words and actions, or lack of actions, pulling me down. But am I strong in solitude? I have strong days, but that's more down to my new sheer bloody-mindedness rather than being alone. Is that what it means? Never giving up on yourself? Solitude is certainly more peaceful. Without arguments festering, it leaves more brain space to think of good things, more productive things.

Solitude has taught me that I don't *need* to be with anyone, especially someone wrong for me, but I don't want to be alone. I know what I want, or, more specifically, who I want. My heart rate shoots up at this thought. *Keep walking, keep going.*

Focus, Cally. Work. What can I say about the resort that I didn't mention the first time around? Whose stupid idea was it to write a second review? Or promise it would bring about world peace?

I crunch through the snow, looking around for inspiration. Did I mention the sanctuary of the Secret Garden before? What parent doesn't need a little down time? And it seems even more peaceful covered in snow. Although, today's serenity is so loud, a constant flow of thoughts echoing through my mind.

Tension accompanies me with every step I take down the path. And robins. Three of them flying around, like they're keeping watch. Their little red breasts standing out against the white backdrop. I'm walking in a Christmas card.

And there it is! The old wishing well. I knew I hadn't been specific enough with my wishes before. I needed to add 'available and close by'. I found him; I just couldn't be with him. Until today. I need coins, stat.

My fingers tremble taking the coins from the bottom of my bag. Ha! There's the same button – that never got sewn on before the coat was donated to the charity shop. Maybe I should clear out my bag more often, or even treat myself to a new one. One day. But right now, I've got wishes to make.

I throw in a handful of coins.

'I wish for... all the things I wished for last time – namely, Jisung – plus for him to be available and within touching, I mean, kissing distance. And to still want me. And inspiration for the perfect words when I see him, and for this work assignment I'm supposed to be thinking about. And for Lexi to have fun. Oh, and for my books to be successful. And somewhere to live would be good.' I lean forward and see the glint of all the coins down at the bottom of the well. So many wishes. I wonder how many have come true?

There's just enough time to cross the little bridge to the centre of the Secret Garden. The moat is frozen – I hope the fishes are safe. There's a familiar scent on the other side, and I follow my nose to find its source. I spot the small white and yellow winter honeysuckle flowers that I recognise from my old garden. Now Ben's garden.

I inhale the sweet fragrance. So much has changed since the last time I smelled these. There's still a long way to go, but life is far better now. Lexi's better off too – not living in a hostile environment hearing arguments. Watching her dad be an asshole. Watching her mum suffer.

Around the corner in the middle of the little island, I find a single red rose in a glass dome. This is something from Beauty and the Beast, but I haven't read that story for a long time and can't remember what it means. I'll have to look it up later.

The rose brings back memories of Jisung at the summer ball. I swore to myself I wouldn't cry, yet here I am with tears in my eyes. I think they're tears of excitement. Or terror. Maybe relief. I don't think there's any chance of calming down now that it's almost lunchtime.

I turn to head back to the hotel in case he comes back early and, in my haste, stumble and fall. Tripping over what? Fresh air? I land on my hands and knees in the snow, soaking my jeans and gloves. A few more steps and I would have fallen into the moat. What is it with this place and me falling? Falling head over heels! Ha! I snort at the silly way my mind works.

I shake myself off, imagining my lovely Barney dog covered in snow and shaking himself. He would love scampering along here, rolling around making doggy snow angels. I miss him already.

I remember walking back this way in the summer – Jisung and I both holding Lexi's hands – and my mind switches from reflective to plain annoying. *Memories… la la la la la moonlight…* I don't know the words or how the rest of the song goes. Just this one line goes through my head on repeat. *Gah!*

On my way to the hotel, I grab a takeaway coffee from the cafe where I met Taylor for that useless interview with 'Cinderella'. Each slow sip warms me from the inside out, bringing heavenly caffeinated respite from the winter chill Ah, the magical powers of caffeine, my trusted ally in the battle against bitter temperatures and nonsensical interviews. If only it could grant me the ability to stop tripping over invisible obstacles. Perhaps my clumsiness is nature's way of reminding me not to take myself too seriously. Well played, universe. Well played.

***

I position myself inside the hotel doorway to keep watch. I'm not sure if lunchtime will mean twelve or two o'clock, or even if he will come this way. My heart rate speeds and I can't stop fidgeting. Watching. Waiting.

After one o'clock, my breathing is back to normal, my legs ache, and I'm sorely tempted to scroll through my phone.

By two o'clock, I give in and have to go to the bathroom. I use the opportunity to have a quick freshen up with a couple of sprays of a random perfume and mouthwash.

Back in position by the lobby window, I watch people coming and going. Long brown fur coats and hats, with large sunglasses, seems to be the dress code for women of a certain age and social status. Then a man on a skidoo pulls up outside, sending a spray of snow as he glides to a stop, much like a car speeding through a puddle. Could it be him?

I can't contain my excitement, and burst out of the door, my heart pounding in my chest. And then, in that moment, he takes off his sunglasses. Is it? Oh my… it… is him! My Prince Charming!

Time stands still as I freeze to the spot, unable to tear my gaze away. It's as if the world around me fades into the background, leaving only him in sharp focus. My heart melts to slush, overwhelmed by the realisation that after all this time, he is right there, in the flesh, at the bottom of the staircase.

Emotion wells up inside me, my eyes brimming with tears of joy and longing. Hand on my chest, I feel the erratic beats of my heart trying to leap from my body. The carefully rehearsed words I had prepared for this moment vanish into thin air, replaced by an overwhelming flood of feelings. This is it. This is the moment I've been waiting for.

Summoning all my courage, my legs trembling beneath me, I take a step forward. But, in a cruel twist of fate, I catch a glimpse of long, blonde hair swaying in the breeze. It's Abbi. No, no, no! She's walking towards Jisung. This is not the moment for her to be here. This is my time, my long-awaited reunion with Jisung. I desperately want it to be ours alone, without an audience or becoming the talk of the resort.

Another shaky step forward, and my heart sinks further. She's stopped to talk to him.

Wait...

My breath catches as she wraps her arms around his neck. The world around me blurs, my vision clouded by tears.

She's about to kiss him.

Unable to bear another second, I spin around, my body trembling with disbelief and utter devastation. My heart shatters into a million pieces, mirroring the delicate snowflakes gently falling around us.

TUESDAY

Plan B

Accept the truth with grace and walk away with dignity. Learn and grow from the experience; acknowledge the pain and remember it will pass. You are strong.

Or some other psychobabble shit I imagine my therapist would say. I scream into my pillow and cry on my bed for two hours straight.

Of course I know I had built up this fantasy into the biggest love story of all time. I wanted the dream so badly I tried to will it into existence. It's hard for an over-thinker and pessimist to be surprised – my mind has already run through every possible scenario. So of course I knew it was possible he could be with someone else. But I had never considered it could be Abbi.

I crawl from the bed and slump on the shaggy rug under the glittering Christmas tree. I search through the piles of scrunched wrapping paper to find the mini liqueur bottles that Lexi unwrapped earlier. With trembling hands, I open the first one and gulp it down in one go. The pain is unbearable.

But now I have to put *Plan B* into operation. The survival plan I had prayed I wouldn't need. But at least now I know. No more wondering, no more doubt, no more dreams.

I allowed myself two hours to cry, to mourn the end. And that's it, no more. Now I have to pack up those feelings and bury them deep inside, never to be seen again. That thought alone chokes me, but I've become a master at hiding feelings – that's what I do best. I cannot, will not, cry forever. And I'll deal with the future when I get home. Well, Mother's home. I must put Lexi first.

I shake back my hair and sit up straight, taking a deep breath. I remember once reading something like *grieving is the price you pay for loving*. But I don't have time to grieve. Mums during Christmas week don't have time to run through every what if and if only. I have to keep going. And there are only so many tears I can cry over losing a man who was never mine.

Jisung is with Abbi now. I have to accept that, even if it kills me inside. Maybe even work towards being happy for my friends that they're together. Although right now, that's asking way too much of myself; my wounds are raw and I need time to heal.

These past months, I have worked so hard to pick up all my broken parts and piece myself back together bit by bit. I have held on by my fingertips to keep mine and Lexi's lives together – through all the times I thought I would fall, and the dark occasions I wanted to let go. For my own sanity, I refuse to let that time go to waste. I cannot crumble again. Lexi is my priority, and I won't let my pain ruin Christmas for her, especially when it's the first one without her dad around. I drink the other five piddly mouthfuls of alcohol and take a shower, determined to cleanse myself of the grief that threatens to consume me.

Plan B, Phase 1, complete.

As I sit at the dressing table applying some concealer to hide my red eyes, my stomach growls. How come when I'm here, with the most delicious eat-as-much-as-I-like food available, I keep missing meal times? I have to keep my strength up. I must go and grab Lexi and find something to eat.

I walk down the grand staircase, trying to enjoy the marvellous decorations, trying to think of the review – the reason we're here. But actually, acknowledging Phase 1 was probably the easiest. It's all very well devising plans in advance, but following them in real life is a different matter. Phase 2: Avoiding Jisung, may be near impossible. He's a lead character at his place of work, where I am staying. And one of Lexi's favourite people here.

Happy mask on, I psyche myself up to head outside and find where Lexi is playing snow games. I walk through the lobby and stand at the cloakroom to get my boots. I pause for a moment, my insides churning, then turn and go to the small hotel bar.

'Good afternoon, Madam. What can I get for you?' asks the tall, slim barman.

'Um… champagne, I suppose.' Not that I'm celebrating, but it's free. 'And do you have any bar snacks, please?'

'Coming right up.' Service with a smile. I wonder whether he's one of the guys who sneaks out drinks for the staff parties? The parties Abbi goes to. Where she tries to kiss the boys for points.

Whether it's hunger or the thought of her kissing Jisung, nausea strikes. Damn, this is hard. How do I face him? Or her? Or even worse still, them together? I can't hide in my room all week.

I glance around at the small, darkened seating area, my eyes drawn to the bright blue lights around the bottles behind the bar. There are minimal touches of elegant Christmas décor – specifically placed baubles and candles for a sophisticated, festive touch. The opposite of how we would usually decorate at home, where it usually looks as though there has been a colour- and glitter-bomb explosion.

I sit on a barstool, the only customer in here, with jolly Christmas music playing softly in the background to taunt me. All the other guests will be enjoying their holiday, playing with their children. I have to pull myself together. *Please, Christmas spirit, I really need you now.*

With a kind smile, the barman passes my drink and a small plate of assorted snacks.

'Ooh, nibbles, my favourite! Thank you.' I smile back. *That's it, Cally. You can do this.* OK, the plan of action: find the children, grab Lexi, go to the restaurant. Easy.

The nibbles taste so good; there's something about a selection of mini salty morsels that acts as an instant mood booster, and I don't leave a single crumb. I finish my drink and take a few deep breaths. I thank the barman again as I drop down from the stool and walk back to the lobby.

Thalia's behind the reception desk and hurries over to me with a heart-warming smile.

'Cally! How are you? Are you feeling better now?'

'I'm fine, thank–'

'If you're looking for Lexi, they've all just gone to dinner in the main restaurant. I'll walk over with you.'

'Thank you.' Thalia is a blessing; her kindness and professionalism make her a real asset to the resort. 'How have things been here? Lots of changes, I hear.'

'Yes, poor Mr Todgers being taken ill. It's been quite a shock to everyone. Mrs Todgers is doing a wonderful job though, and I've been helping her as much as I can.'

We're almost at the restaurant and my heart rate quickens. I must keep talking to keep my nerves at bay. I want to ask what she knows about *things*, but daren't. 'Do you like the management side of things?'

'I really do. Guests are lovely, of course.' She smiles and pats my back. 'But I enjoy working with the staff. Especially the younger ones who are living away from home for the first time. Sometimes they need a little more support.'

'Ah, yes, I've seen a few new younger faces.'

We arrive at the restaurant and my body tenses. He's likely to be inside. My stomach is in knots and I've lost my appetite. Thalia opens the door. 'Let's find Lexi.'

The huge restaurant is decorated as an indoor winter wonderland and is packed with tables full of hungry guests. I glance around to find Lexi, but instead my eyes immediately pick him out of the crowd. His head of black hair towers above the guests he's seated with. My heart stammers. He looks exactly as I remember, yet feels like a stranger. I clench Thalia's arm to steady myself, and keep my eyes down, thankful she is here with me.

'I see her.' Thalia points further ahead and taps the shoulder of a nearby host. 'Please can we have an extra setting at the end of table nine?'

Each step fills me with dread that he'll look up and see me. That we'll lock eyes across the crowded space, emotions laid bare. But his focus stays fixed ahead, unaware. I am so relieved Lexi's sitting several tables away from him, and by the time we get to her table, an extra place setting has been laid out next to hers. I thank Thalia and take a seat.

'Mum! We've had so much fun today!'

A winter wonderland cocktail is placed on the snow-themed table in front of me. 'Fantastic! Tell me all about it.' Bubbly Lexi is exactly what I need to keep me focused.

'What did we do first?' she asks her new friends sitting beside her.

'Snowball fight!'

'Snowmen!'

'Sledding!'

The noisy chaos makes me laugh. Five children, all loud and animated, all talking at the same time. I share several looks with their parents down the table. I think we all agree it's great they've had a good day, and much as we love them, my goodness, they talk non-stop! The children don't pause, even when the food arrives. They just continue with the new exciting topic of conversation.

The servers place white sharing plates with a variety of white foods down on the tables between mini Christmas trees and snowmen. Aha! Hidden vegetables time! Mini cups of white soup... parsnip? Cauliflower maybe? Snowflake-shaped tortillas with white dip... feta? It's a tantalising feast of mini white dishes bursting with disguised goodness. Lexi tries all kinds of foods she never would normally and refuses to believe the yummy tower of white contains fish and other ingredients she claims to hate.

It is lovely Lexi's made some friends, and their chatter is the perfect accessory to Phase 2. But then the feta dip reminds me Jisung said he didn't like cheese and I make the mistake of glancing up. I am in his direct eye line. I twist in my seat, head ducking low behind other diners to keep out of view. My body sways each time one of them moves so I stay covered.

Whereas I've now felt the shock of three brief sightings, unless he's seen Lexi, he doesn't even know I'm here. Thankfully, surrounded by guests, Prince Charming can't be seen to have any kind of personal scene with a guest – good or bad – so I can avoid an awkward conversation. Awkward for me anyway. My reality is he's gone back on his wish, broken my heart, and destroyed my dreams. His reality is that he's simply living his life.

I am sitting next to one of Lexi's new friends, Joe. I can feel him staring as I continue to bob around in my seat. I am aiming to stay hidden behind a large woman sitting on a table between me and Jisung. But she won't sit still, which means neither can I. Joe loudly whispers, 'Lexi, what's wrong with your mum?'

'Ugh, I can't take her anywhere. She's so embarrassing.' I can hear Lexi's eyes roll with her response.

Ignoring my daughter's conversation, I look up as the servers bring our desserts. That's when we make fleeting eye contact. He may not have been consciously looking at me, but I feel my cheeks flame. After all, I have, in effect, been dumped for another woman. And not only does that hurt, it's humiliating to be cast aside for someone better. Thoughts flood my mind, but I actively tell them to stop. I think I may have learned something in therapy after all.

I refocus my attention on the exquisite meringue shapes arriving at our table and quickly sit upright. Unaware of the server behind my chair, my head crashes into her metal tray and a loud clang vibrates through my ears. Tiny pieces of crushed meringue snow down over me and Joe. I sigh and sit in stunned silence, keeping my eyes down while the commotion happens around me.

That's right, folks. Cally Jackson is back in town.

Joe screeches, 'It's snowing!' while his younger brother picks the pieces from his hair and eats them. Lexi has disappeared under the table as her friends all laugh. The waitress is apologising and running off to get replacements. My anarchic, disobedient eyes glance up to see a great many faces turned my way. And this time, he is definitely looking at me – eyes wide, mouth open. I immediately look down before horror reaches his face.

With no point hiding any longer, I stand and shake off the avalanche of white crumbs. I curtsy and smile politely to signify the end of the *Cally Show*, allowing everyone to continue with their meals and stop gawping. I ignore the shade Lexi is throwing and sit back down to eat a small meringue snowman.

The only thing I can think about is that although that man looks like Jisung, he is not the same man I have been dreaming of. I am in love with the Jisung from my memories – the fantasy Jisung, who is not the real-life man sitting over there. He is the one who is with Abbi.

All things considered, I think I am coping quite well. I imagine my therapist patting me on the back. Even if I am counting down the minutes until I can release the tears that are struggling to wait patiently.

An announcement is made at the end of dinner – we have visitors from the North Pole outside. Children surge towards the door in a frenzy of excited cheers and squeals.

'Meet you outside!' I call to Lexi, along with similar yells from all the other parents left at the back of the queue. Avoidance plan in operation, I use the rush as cover to exit the dining hall and dive into the lobby washroom.

I lock myself in a cubicle, and tears stream down my face. Hell, I know it wasn't love in the summer. But it was something. And now it is nothing. And it hurts more than my marriage ending, because at least Ben and I gave it a good go. Jisung and I never had a chance to try. While I thought of him every single day, he couldn't wait for me. *He* never gave us a chance. And went off with Abbi of all people. How are they compatible?

I hear the squeak of someone opening the bathroom door. I can't stay in here all evening. I must go outside to Lexi, even if I am the biggest embarrassment ever. I dry my eyes and open the cubicle door. Diane is standing in front of the mirror, adjusting her hair, and our eyes meet in its reflection.

'Cally? What's wrong?' Diane spins around and puts her hand on my shoulder.

I splash water over my face and sob, 'I'm fine… thank you.'

'You don't look fine, dear. Tell me.'

'Oh, you know, relationship ending. Losing someone is difficult.' I pat my face dry and look around for a miracle product for puffy eyes.

'He will regret losing you. Don't fret over things you can't change now. You hold your beautiful head high, dear, and remember you're a strong woman who'll be just fine without him.' She pushes the hair from my face with a comforting smile. She believes in me. Now I need to believe in myself.

I pull back my shoulders. 'You're right, Diane. I will be fine without him.'

'Now come. There's some lovely huskies outside.' She opens the door and we go to collect our boots. I can't stay sad with a daughter and doggies waiting for me.

***

It's hectic outside, with guests huddling around the dogs and a line of torch-lit sledges pulled by a team of huskies, ready to take off. A yell from one of the sledges catches my attention.

'Mum! Quick!'

'Cally!'

Lexi is in a sledge and there beside her is none other than Jisung, and they have saved me a space. Shit.

I run closer and call out to Lexi that I'll meet her when they get back. She smiles and waves and then they're off. Jisung turns back with a huge smile. He holds out his hand, crossing his index finger and thumb to form a finger heart. I stop still, perplexed, and immediately look around to see if Abbi is standing behind me. But it's only Diane standing there, saying, 'I think he missed you.'

I stare after them.

'Do you want to come back inside, Cally?'

'N-no... I want to see the dogs...'

'OK, dear. I'll see you in a while.' Diane pauses before walking away. 'Will you be all right?'

I nod and slowly traipse towards one of the dog crowds.

Firstly, what the...?

Secondly, although that wasn't planned, it has actually worked out well. I'm not a suitable candidate for a sledge ride. I would scream the whole way and frighten the dogs, and then there would be another snowy meringue-type disaster, but on a catastrophic dog/sledge/people/avalanche scale that doesn't bear thinking about. While I love to *look* at snow, participating in snow activities is not really my cup of tea.

Thirdly, now what?

I wait in the queue to meet one of the huskies, allowing the children to cut in line before me while I think of a new plan. OK, when they come back, I grab Lexi and we run. Sorted.

Eventually, it's my turn to meet Nala. She's friendly and gorgeous and I need the calm of stroking her thick fur. I miss my Barney dog cuddles.

By the time I've drunk a few glasses of mulled wine to warm up, the distant jingling of bells alerts me to the husky ride returning. The sound sends a nervous shiver through me. I walk back over to their arrival area, heart in my throat, and get ready to grab and run.

When Lexi skips over to me, however, she doesn't want to be grabbed. She wriggles out of my clutches and runs off to pet the dogs, leaving me standing alone. I panic, not quite sure which way to run, and turn to head inside. That's when it hits me. A perfectly aimed ball of snow to the back of my head. I yelp at the shock of impact and the freezing wet lump sliding down my neck. But I hurry onwards.

'Cally?'

I pretend not to hear, my heart thumping like crazy, and speed ahead.

A hand grabs the forearm of my coat, but it's loose enough to shake off. Then I am grabbed by the wrist and swung around. I stop breathing. There's no escaping the moment.

I swing around into his arms but push him away at the same time. I daren't look up to his face.

'Cally?' He takes me in his arms again. 'I can't believe you're really here!' The delight ringing in his voice pains me like a dagger in my heart. He hugs me tightly, but my arms remain by my side. I'm determined not to cry.

'Are you OK? Cally?' He gently turns my cheek to make me look at him. 'What's happened?'

'I saw you earlier.' The words burst from my mouth. 'With Abbi.'

'I don't understand.'

I stare at him in disbelief. 'She flung herself at you!' My eyes fill with tears, my throat straining to contain the ball of emotion.

'Ah, yes, she did,' he says in his matter-of-fact tone. I look into his eyes, his beautiful, kind eyes, which pains my broken heart even more. He makes no apology, no excuses.

'And did you see what happened next?' He strokes the back of my wet head.

I shake away his touch, the tenderness only twisting the hurt deeper. I can't be comforted by the person causing my pain. 'I came back to you as soon as I could.' I choke out my words. 'But you didn't wait for me.'

Tears of gullibility spill down my cheeks. He holds my face in his hand and wipes my tears with his thumb. 'Cally, I stepped away.'

I freeze, my mind blanking in shock. No, that can't be right. I clearly saw…

A line etches between his brows. 'Abbi is not part of my life.'

'I hoped you wouldn't forget me.' My voice breaks, and I turn my head away. 'Like I never forgot you…'

'Please look at me.' He speaks softly and waits until I reluctantly look back at him. His beautiful, gentle face looks confused and concerned, which messes with my head. But even if there's an explanation, it's too late. The damage is already done.

'There's nothing between me and Abbi.' He puts his hand over his heart. 'I didn't forget you, believe me.'

His expression is sincere, insistent, and I want to believe him so much. I want him to hold me. He sounds genuine, but I'm not a fool. I saw her arms around him. I saw her about to kiss him.

'Let me prove it to you, Cally.' His eyes search mine with pleading intensity. 'Let me take you on a date, tomorrow evening. Let me show you what you can believe.'

I blink away muddled tears; I don't want to cry again. I must be strong. 'I'll have to think about it.'

He puts his arm around my back, leans in, and gives me a long kiss on my forehead – a bittersweet gesture that serves as a haunting reminder of what has been lost. I daren't close my eyes and give myself to his kiss. I step back before my chest explodes. 'I have to get Lexi to bed.'

'It's so good to see you.' He strokes my arm as I walk away. 'I will see you tomorrow. Please look forward to it.'

WEDNESDAY

Dream Come True

Whether it's too much caffeine or the freezing temperatures, my hands are either trembling or shivering; standing in the snow is not how I'm used to starting the day. It was almost impossible to walk past the comfy-looking armchairs around the fireplace to come outside instead of curling up in the warm. But it's fun-mum time.

All the children are bundled up, jumping around in the snow like penguins with their parents in tow, waiting for details of the morning's activities. I can only recognise Lexi by her bright fuchsia woollen hat.

An orange-suited leader calls for the guests' attention.

'Good morning, everyone!' He puts his hand to his ear. A few children echo his greeting.

'I can't hear you…'

'Good morning,' mumble a few more guests.

'Come on, parents, you can do better than that!' Orange Man laughs. 'No hiding in the back there. I see you! Good morning, everyone!'

'Good morning,' we all reply. It seems we're part of a pantomime. How tiresome.

'We have an exciting morning planned for you all.' The children all cheer; the parents, not so much. 'We're starting with a winter wonderland scavenger hunt! Hidden in the gardens are many surprises… Bring your treasures to the yurt at midday, where we'll all meet for lunch and prizes!'

The children cheer again.

'I can't hear you…'

I'm too grumpy first thing in the morning to cope with Orange Man. 'Woohoooo!' I yell, minus enthusiasm. You can tell which guests are British by their reserved reluctance to cheer as loudly and enthusiastically as some of the others.

'But…' Orange Man throws his hand in the air. 'You must watch out for the cheeky elves – if they catch you, they might take one of your treasures to keep for themselves!'

The children gasp. Uh oh, I fear there may be tears ahead (they may well be mine). And running. Ugh. Let's hope the snow puts an end to the idea of such exertion.

The fairy-tale cast members join the crowd – each one cleverly dressed in snowsuit costumes. It makes sense that the princesses wouldn't want to prance around in their dresses in this weather.

Orange Man claps his hands. 'Everyone needs to be in a group of at least three people. Hands up if you need someone to join you.'

Lexi jumps up and down, hands waving in the air. She runs through the crowd and returns moments later with her scavenger hunt bag and a third person to join our group.

'Good morning, Cally. Are you ready to have some fun?' Prince Charming winks at me. With a tentative smile, I feel a sudden rush of heat which culminates in my cheeks. I look away and hear his familiar chuckle. I am not mentally prepared. This was not part of my plan. I don't yet know if I believe he's not with Abbi, and I haven't had a chance to see her. I certainly don't yet know if I want to go on a date with him, let alone spend a few hours playing now, trying to act normally in front of Lexi.

I take the scavenger bag from Lexi's hand and fumble through, pleased to have something to make myself look busy. Thank goodness Lexi babbles incessantly, lapping up his attention, until she sees Baby Bear wearing a snowman costume. 'Hi, Hannah!' she calls out loudly, waving across the crowd.

'Lexi!' I hiss through gritted teeth. 'Don't spoil it for the younger kids.'

'Oops! Sorry.' She pulls her hat down almost over her eyes and ducks her head – for all of two seconds, before excitement makes her bounce up again.

Why couldn't she have picked Baby Bear to join us? Why does Prince Charming have to be her favourite?

I glance up to see Jisung's flirty smile. His gaze makes me feel shy and I lower my head, feeling half giddy and half… jealous… of Abbi.

I retreat into my shell. His smile tangles my thoughts further and does nothing to soothe my aching heart. Our time together in the summer meant something to me, even without the physical intimacy, and despite how ridiculous it seems after something so short-lived. I thought he felt the same. And now the thought that I was just a casual fling, that he could move on with ease into the arms of someone else, knocks my confidence in any potential *us*. And I don't know if there is any coming back from that.

I can feel my thoughts spiralling out of control, but deep down I know the real issue. Fear. Specifically, the fear that I'm not good enough for him.

I can't compete with Abbi. And I don't want to; she's my friend, and she's done nothing wrong. Still, I find myself fighting the urge to hate her – but I know that's jealousy. She's young and pretty. I know she wanted him and would have been an easy catch. But he could have any woman he wants. Why her? Then again, why would he ever choose me?

Today, I'll have to put on the greatest acting performance of my lifetime.

And... action.

Families disperse in all directions. Lexi and Prince Charming walk off, and I slip and slide behind. He leads us towards the Secret Garden, but turns off just before. It's hard to tell which garden is which when they're all white. I feel a little bit grateful he's with us so we don't get lost. I haven't had a chance to buy a flare gun yet.

The path looks like a movie set – lined with snow-covered trees either side, bright sunshine finding its way through the low-hanging branches that we weave through, crunching footprints in the freshly fallen snow. My darling daughter skips merrily ahead, hand in hand with the beautiful man I have been dreaming of for so long. It would be the perfect scene, if I knew I could trust him.

But he's the acting pro here, an award-winning actor at that, used to making people believe what he says in any situation. I have to protect myself; I'm too old and weary to go through more drama. I just want an easy, peaceful life. Don't I? Back at the wishing well, didn't I wish for fun and excitement and adventure? Maybe I can't have it all ways.

I need to get my head back in the game. 'Guys, team meeting.'

Lexi and Jisung stop and turn around. I hold out the scavenger hunt list. 'We need to look at what treasures to collect.'

'Me! Me! I want to read it!'

I hand the list to Lexi and her pout deepens as she reads through the list. 'Pinecone, red berries, holly, acorn? These aren't treasures.'

'They are nature's treasures. There is magic and beauty all around when you take time to notice.' Jisung takes Lexi's hand and leads her through the trees. I quickly follow so I don't get left behind. 'This bush here, do you know what it is?' Lexi shakes her head. 'This is a holly bush. Who do you think eats these berries?' She points up to a bird in the tree.

Jisung nods. 'Some people believe holly brings good luck, especially tomorrow. Do you know what day it is?'

'Thursday!' Lexi smiles, looking smug that she knows the answer.

'It is also the winter solstice – the shortest day and longest night of the year. In Korea, we call it *Dongji*, and we celebrate with a special red bean porridge.'

'Yuck!'

I shoot Lexi a look.

'Sorry. I don't like beans.' Then her mouth falls open. 'If it's the shortest day, does that mean I have to go to bed earlier?'

Before Jisung can reply, we hear jingling bells.

Lexi's eyes open wide. She sticks out her arms to halt us and whispers, 'Hide!'

The three of us crouch behind the holly bush, all stifling our giggles.

'Give me a treat! Give me a treat! And I will give you something to eat!'

Lexi can't resist taking a peep and squeals, 'It's an elf!'

'Found you!' the elf sings, peering over the top of the bush. We all look up to see a jolly painted face and a green elf hat with a bell at the end. We stand up, laughing.

'Do you have a treat for me?' The elf does a little jig, making Lexi laugh. Jisung quickly picks a holly leaf for her to give him.

'Here you go,' Lexi sings back.

'Ha ha! Thank you! Here is your treat.' He hands Lexi a candy cane. 'Now I shall be on my way. Hope you have a magical day!' And off he skips.

We all laugh, and Jisung picks another holly leaf and some berries for Lexi to put in the bag.

'Let's get some extra ones in case we bump into another elf.' I take off my glove to pick a leaf and prick my finger. 'Ouch!' Jisung takes my hand and holds it tenderly, lifts it to his lips, and kisses my finger better. My eyes flit immediately to Lexi, but she has her back turned. He hasn't let go of my hand.

'You still wear our mushroom house.'

His affectionate smile makes me blush yet again. 'I've never taken it off,' I whisper, and tug my hand away to put my glove back on. I can't acknowledge the pain in his eyes as his smile fades. I look back to Lexi, who has already unwrapped the candy cane and is sucking away, thankfully missing what just happened. I have no idea how she might react to a man, especially Prince Charming, kissing my hand or coming into our lives in any way.

Jisung carefully picks some more holly as Lexi comes closer. 'The elf might have followed our footprints. Perhaps we should stay off the path.'

'Good plan, Prince Charming!' Lexi jumps up and gives him a high-five. We continue on our trek, Lexi and Jisung searching for more treasures, me kicking snow behind them. How dare he be so good with her?

I'm happy to walk behind while the duo in front sing and laugh together. I love watching how carefree and happy Lexi is after all she's been through recently. I have to do what I can to put her life back together, to provide her with some stability. Even if Jisung was telling the truth and was able to win back my trust, where would that leave us? Realistically, what could the future possibly hold with us living so far apart?

As we climb a steep incline, the cold air hits the back of my throat and makes me cough. But when we get to the top, the view is awe-inspiring. Even Lexi is unusually quiet. Nature – pristine, undisturbed, dormant. There is hushed stillness and serenity in the air, like time has stopped, and the thick cover of snow muffles the chaos of the outside world. The white landscape sparkles in the sunlight like it's sprinkled with glitter, and we can see the Christmas lights shining around the resort – an enchanting scene and breathtakingly beautiful.

I close my eyes and breathe deeply, hoping the tranquillity will permeate my brain to finally bring some calm. In these few moments, I feel cleansed and revitalised. I feel free. A rush of warmth and happiness flows through me as the sunshine warms my face and makes me smile. I want to put out my arms and spin around and delight in my new-found freedom.

When I open my eyes, Jisung is looking at me affectionately, and for that fleeting moment I feel our connection again. Like our souls reuniting, pure, without any interruption from thoughts or plans or worries. I shake the over-romanticised nonsense from my mind. Was he watching me the whole time I had my eyes closed?

I look around to find Lexi, who has scampered off and found winter jasmine. As I walk towards her, there's a nudge against my back. Jisung has put his hand on top of all my layers to walk with me. Today could have been so different if I hadn't seen that moment of him and Abbi together. I pull away from his arm with a warning side glance, and a defeated look crosses his face. It makes me want to reach out to him. But he's an actor. I can't trust what I see. He wants me to not believe what I saw with my own eyes.

I rush to Lexi and smell the jasmine, but it has no fragrance. She picks a few flowers and puts them in the bag.

'Come, Lexi. I want to show you something.' Jisung takes her hand and she skips away.

'What? What is it?'

'It's one of the resort's hidden treasures.'

We change direction and head through the trees, uphill again.

'How on earth do you remember the layout of this place? It's huge!' I ask, forgetting I am supposed to be cross and upset. If I actually hated him, this would be so much easier.

I don't really hear his answer; instead, I hear my own words in my head. *Stop playing games. I am a grown woman, not a teenager. This trust issue goes both ways; he won't get to know me either if I'm not being my true self. Just quit it.* I'm caught off guard by my telling off. It takes a moment to pull myself together, but then I remember I'm Fun Mum and run to catch up.

'Is it far?' My legs are starting to feel heavy.

'We're nearly at the edge of the woods.' He turns to me with a grin and steps away for me to walk alongside them both.

'Please can I walk in the middle?' Lexi asks as she barges between us with a beaming smile, taking hold of our gloves. 'Now it's like we're a family. You can pretend to be my stepdad, Prince Charming, and then I can be a princess.'

Jisung and I exchange glances. He laughs, whereas I wince at the awkwardness. Good old Lex. She can always be relied on to embarrass me.

Once we have passed through the trees, the landscape transforms entirely. We are met with a wide-open expanse of pristine snow and clear blue skies. Squinting against the bright glare, I understand now why sunglasses were among our gifts. Towering icy structures loom ahead, resembling massive squared-off boulders, with a pathway winding through them.

'Oh no! Not a maze?' I'm reminded of my last disastrous maze encounter.

'No. Lexi, any guesses?'

Her eyes light up. 'Um… ice trolls?'

'Good guess! This is the realm of the Ice Queen.'

Lexi gasps and grabs our arms. 'Is she scary?'

'No one has ever survived to tell the tale.'

A mix of fear and fascination dances across Lexi's face. Jisung keeps the drama up by dropping his voice to a hoarse whisper. 'We have to be quiet because she despises being disturbed.'

With the spark of imagination in her eyes, Lexi takes a deep breath, looking thrilled at the prospect of adventure.

We weave through ice structures – uphill, my poor legs – and come to a long, tall wall of ice. It's how I imagine a frozen waterfall might look, and glistening in the sunshine, it's a stunning sight. I can't tell if it's real or not, but it's certainly an impressive hidden treasure we're fortunate to find. One Lexi and I wouldn't have stumbled upon without our expert guide.

'Shhhh!' Jisung warns, and the three of us creep through the snow towards what looks like an icy awning.

'What happens if she catches us?' Lexi's eyes are wide and she clutches on to us tightly.

'Legend has it that she locks people up in her ice dungeon!'

Lexi's gasp echoes through the wintry air.

The cave entrance is dripping with long, sparkling icicles that continue inside, where it's dimly lit with a shadowy blue glow.

'Now we have a decision to make!' Prince Charming drops to his knee to speak quietly with Lexi. 'I hear there is something very special on the other side of the cave.'

'The hidden treasure?' Her little voice trembles – I'm not sure if it's from excitement or trepidation, or maybe both.

'That's right. Do we dare enter?'

She looks up at me with big eyes. 'Mum, are you brave enough to go in?' I try not to laugh. That wasn't what I expected her to say. She turns to Jisung. 'You'll make sure my mum's safe, won't you, Prince Charming?'

He stands up with his hand on his heart. 'I will always make sure you and your mum are safe.'

'Come on then, Mum. We'll look after you.' Lexi leads the way, and Jisung gives me a wink. I admit I'm glad he came with us; he's made today extra special for Lexi.

We duck down and slink our way through the cave, my heart thumping in case a troll does jump out at us. Turning at the end, we see a stream of daylight ahead. Lexi puts up her fist to make us stop and turns to us with a whisper. 'OK, we must be very quiet and peep around the corner to see if it's clear.' Jisung and I share a silent chuckle. Lexi peeks her head out and calls back, 'It's all clear. Go, go, go!'

We creep out the back of the cave into an icy courtyard with a gate to one side.

'Quick, follow me!' My brave, young adventurer waves us forward. Jisung unhooks the gate and we follow Lexi through, finding ourselves on a path surrounded by frosty bushes and trees covered in twinkling icicle lights. A little further ahead, Lexi stops and raises her hand to her ear. 'Bells! Hide!' In an instant, Lexi dives behind a nearby bush, while Jisung pulls me in the opposite direction.

Jisung nudges me behind a large tree, his hand firmly anchored beside my head. My breath catches in my throat as he blocks me against the trunk. I blink back at the wicked glint in his eyes, my heart racing.

He leans in closer, our cheeks lightly touching, and whispers into my ear, 'I've missed you, Cally.' His breath is warm and fast against my neck and my back arches, pushing my chest out to meet his. Protests bounce on my lips, though never make a sound – my god, I want him. This is what I've craved all this time.

He presses closer, his thigh firm between mine, layers of winter clothing doing nothing to hide his arousal. My heart rockets as his lips trail a slow path up my throat, barely grazing my skin. His teasing makes me ache for him all the more desperately. I want him to kiss me, to feel his passion again.

His mouth hovers a breath away from mine, so temptingly close I can almost taste him. We both tremble with longing, our restraint hanging by a thread as I desperately try to stifle a moan that threatens to escape out loud.

But this isn't right. I push him back forcefully, the loss of his touch like a physical ache. 'I can't do this,' I gasp. Although I want to do this more than anything, I can't betray Abbi when I could be here with her boyfriend.

We don't break eye contact while we both attempt to catch our breath. I can't help the smile tugging at the corner of my mouth. 'You remembered.'

He runs his hand through his hair and smirks. 'You were right. That was hot as hell.' I give him a playful nudge, feeling a little pink in the cheeks.

Being almost-kissed up against a tree was even more steamy than I always dreamed it would be. Though I wonder if this is what Fairy-Tale Wonderland has in mind when they promise to make dreams come true.

'Please say you'll come on a date with me this evening.' His beautiful dark eyes plead with me. I'm not sure which of my body parts makes the decision, but I nod.

'Mum!' Lexi whispers loudly. 'They didn't catch us!'

We emerge from behind the tree and she runs over, pulling us all into a celebratory hug. Above Lexi's head, Jisung gives me a flirty smile and I have to look away. I'm still trying to come to terms with agreeing to a date. As well as recover from the sensation of those lips on my neck.

'The danger's not over,' Jisung whispers, falling back into character. 'We still need to get to the far end.'

As we near the end gate, an elf leaps onto the path in front of us. Lexi and I both scream and then burst into fits of laughter. The elf apologises for making us jump so violently by giving Lexi a snowman lollipop without asking for treasure in return. As we walk on, the elf pats Jisung on the shoulder. Beneath their costumes, they must be friends.

'Hey!' the elf calls from behind, and the three of us turn around. 'I hear the Ice Queen is nearby. Watch out!' He laughs and jingles off. Lexi tries to blink away the sudden fear in her eyes.

Prince Charming tries to amp up the tension. 'This is the final gate. Do you think we can make it without being caught?'

Lexi gives a nonchalant shrug. 'Of course. Follow me.' She unhooks the gate and we file through. Before us is a long ice slide.

'We found the treasure!' She cheers and grabs a mat ready to go. However, I stumble backwards and feel the colour drain from my face.

'What's wrong, Mum?'

'It's too steep! I'm terrified.'

'You'll be fine,' she sings. 'It's fun!' And off she whizzes down the icy slope, rounding the bend at the end to who knows where?

'Please tell me there's another way down?' I beg, edging back to the gate.

'Only back the way we came.' Jisung puts his arms around me. 'I'll keep you safe, remember?' He reaches down to collect a larger mat. 'I've got you.' He sits on the mat at the top of the slope and gestures for me to come closer. 'Come between my legs.' I might have childishly giggled at his choice of words had I not been petrified.

With extreme reluctance, I lower myself onto the mat. Jisung puts his arms around me from behind and pushes us off. I clutch on to his legs for dear life, and scream. I scream as we pick up speed, and scream around every bend. But when the bottom comes into sight, I'm able to relax enough to actually laugh. And for that very last tiny part, I even enjoy the adrenaline rush!

When we slide to a stop, Jisung offers me his hand and pulls me to my feet. I throw my arms around him. 'Thank you! I could never have done that without you.'

He hugs me back with a huge grin. 'Anytime.'

Neither of us lets go until a few moments later when Lexi giggles. 'Oooo-ooooh!'

Jisung takes Lexi by the hand, a mischievous grin on his face. 'Let's go and find some lunch.' Lexi reaches out to hold my hand too, and we walk off together in search of food and prizes.

***

Delicious barbecue smells tantalise our empty stomachs as we reach the yurt. Inside, there's a roaring fire in the middle, where staff are busy cooking lunch. It's cosy and warm, and a perfect retreat when I feel frozen to the core. That's the price I pay for buying the cheapest coat for myself so I could afford Lexi the best.

The three of us sit on a bench together, Lexi in the middle, and wrap ourselves in blankets while serving staff brings us big mugs of hot chocolate. I love how the resort anticipates all we might want before we even know ourselves.

Lunchtime is a rustic and relaxed affair. Soon after sitting, the server brings over our plates. 'Fresh reindeer hotdogs for the prince and his lovely ladies. Enjoy.'

Lexi holds out her plate, aghast at the server's announcement. 'Reindeer? Was he joking?'

'Just try it. I'm sure it will be yummy,' I encourage, but it hasn't been cleverly disguised like the vegetables.

'Santa's reindeer?' she asks a little too loudly with other children within hearing distance. Tears begin to fill her eyes.

'How *Rudolph* them to serve reindeer!' Jisung attempts to bring back Lexi's smiles.

I jump in too. 'It's un-brr-lieveable!'

Lexi alternates staring at us both.

'It's *snow* problem. There's plenty of other food.' Jisung attracts the attention of a server. 'We will need some Lexi-friendly food, please.'

The server takes her plate and bows. 'Of course, Your Highness.'

Lexi giggles.

'There, we can all *chill* out now. Different food is on the way.' Jisung smiles. Our pun-derful fun appears to have gone over Lexi's head.

'Are you a real prince?' Lexi goes direct for the information that I expect she's wanted for a long time. This conversation could skirt far too close to which other characters are real. Santa, for example. With such a short time left for her to hold on to her magical beliefs, I look to Jisung to see how this will pan out.

'I am Prince of Fairy-Tale Wonderland, yes.'

She accepts his answer without question and I sigh, relieved. Until her next question.

'Have you got a girlfriend?'

The server interrupts any potential awkwardness, bringing over a plate of reindeer-*shaped* goodies, which meet Lexi's approval.

'So, have you got a girlfriend?' she asks, undeterred by her mouthful of rainbow slaw.

'Lexi! Perhaps we shouldn't ask the prince personal questions?'

'Oh, it's just, I thought, because you and Dad aren't together anymore, perhaps you could–'

'Lexi!'

Ignoring the warning tone of my voice, she whirls around. 'Prince Charming, if you married my mum, would I be a real princess?'

'Lexi!' My daughter has such a way with words that I've stress-crushed a reindeer cookie without realising, and I try to brush away the crumbs before anyone notices. Jisung laughs, Lexi is oblivious, and I am dying. I suppose I should at least be thankful that *she* doesn't have a crush on Prince Charming too, because that would be very awkward indeed. I put my arm around her shoulders and give her a squeeze. 'I glove you snow much, Lex.' I shake my head. That girl!

Jisung squeezes my shoulder, but my attention snaps towards a faint but familiar tune. Lexi spins around, gasping at me. 'Mum, that's your phone!'

I dive at our pile of coats, frantically searching for the right pocket so I can switch off the disturbance. I locate the hard shape through the material and press all the buttons I can feel. After a few seconds of the ringtone getting louder, I manage to make it silent. I daren't look up to see any horrified or annoyed glares.

Covertly unzipping the pocket, I peek at the screen. 'It was your dad, Lex. I better call him back.' I nip outside. After all, I wouldn't want to miss another dire missing-shirt emergency.

'Ben.' We're way beyond pleasantries.

'I'm not signing these divorce papers. I'm not giving you half of what I've worked for. You were the one who walked away. I already gave you everything.'

I sigh. 'No, Ben, all you gave me was trust issues and anxiety.' I try to sound calm. I don't want him to know he can still upset me.

'What the hell do you mean?'

I can picture him spitting his words into the phone, and it makes me shudder. I walk away from the yurt entrance so nobody can hear my humiliation. 'Not forgetting that woman you brought into my house.'

'You were lucky I stayed with you for so long.' His voice is as calm and condescending as ever.

'Was I though?' I start to shiver. Or maybe I'm shaking.

'Don't think you'll ever find anyone else who'll put up with you.'

Save it, Cally. Don't give him the satisfaction. 'Merry Christmas, Ben.'

I hang up and throw the phone down into the snow. Why did he have to call now? I can't deal with him too. I sink my head into my hands as the conversation replays in my mind. I try not to let his words affect me, but I reflexively burst into tears.

Then I jump as my coat is placed around my shoulders and my phone slid back into my pocket. I spin around with a rush of panic, ready to hide my tears from Lexi. Instead I am caught by arms that envelop me, and in that moment of vulnerability, I rest my head on Jisung's chest. My tears drip down his coat, but I'm not upset – each teardrop is a release of anger and fear. How dare Ben make me cry, here and now?

My body is shaking. Jisung loosens his grip and unzips his coat, drawing me to the warmth of his body. He pulls his coat around me, and in his hold, my breathing begins to calm.

'I didn't mean to overhear. I was just bringing out your coat so you didn't freeze.'

Through shuddering breaths, I manage to utter, 'Thank you.'

'Problems at home?'

I wipe my eyes on my sleeve, but as I go to put my arm down again, it seems to slip around his waist of its own accord. I close my eyes. I have too many conflicted emotions to cope with, and some accidentally overspill out loud.

'He won't agree to the divorce, which means he won't sell the house, so I have no money for a home for me and Lexi. I'll have to stay sleeping on my mother's couch. Forever.' I slump back onto Jisung's chest, and he holds me tightly as tears stream down my face again.

'It will be OK, I promise. Somehow, it will all work out.'

His words soothe my crushed spirit, even if my mind doesn't believe them. Ben is trapping me in another cage when I've only just managed to escape.

'I'm sorry, you don't need to hear all my worries.' I drag myself out of Jisung's arms and zip his coat back up. I can't cope with this now, any of it. I roughly wipe away my tears, and Jisung puts his arm around my shoulder.

'You don't need to go through this alone, Cally. I'm here whenever you need to talk.' I look up at his face and find solace. And yet he causes me pain too. How do I pick myself up to be fun Christmas mum when I've made my daughter homeless? How am I supposed to focus on work?

I shove my hands in my pockets, and the cold breeze stings my eyes. I need some time to straighten out my head.

'I'm sorry anyway,' I mumble.

'Don't apologise. I want to be here for you.' Jisung smooths my hair back from my face.

I want to stay in the comfort he willingly gives, but the conflict it brings tears at my insides. I look into his reassuring eyes. 'Please could you do me a favour? Could you tell Lexi that I have to work, and can you find Nanny P to stay with her for the prize-giving?'

'Of course, anything to help.'

I attempt a smile and walk away. I don't know what to do, what to believe. And there may be only one way to find out.

WEDNESDAY

O Christmas Tree

I stand outside the spa entrance for what feels like hours. I even manage to put my hand on the push sign a couple of times. But I just can't do it. I'm torn between wanting to speak to Abbi and not wanting to hear what she says. Before I freeze to the spot, I have to admit defeat. I am a coward. A big, spineless, yellow-bellied, chickening-out, scaredy-cat idiot.

***

Back in the hotel, toes defrosting in warm slippers, I head to reception. Avoiding eye contact with Shana in case she asks for the work I have yet to think about, I drag Thalia to the small bar. She wasn't quite kicking and screaming, but I had to be persistent when asking for her company.

'What's going on?' she asks as I order two winter wonderland cocktails.

'In all honesty,' I sigh, and my head dips, 'I need a friend.'

'Oh!' She sounds surprised, as though she hasn't had this request from a guest before. 'How can I help?'

I'm not even sure what I want from her – she can't change my situation, and I can't go into specifics because of the no-staff-relationships rule. And I'm pretty sure Thalia is a stickler for rules.

'Just sit with me for a while. Please?'

Thalia leans against the bar. 'I can do that. I've been running around all morning, and I could do with a rest.'

The barman sets down our drinks. Thalia takes a sip of her cocktail and giggles, raising her shoulders to her ears. 'This feels very naughty during work time.'

'You wouldn't want me drinking alone, would you?' I join in with her giggles. It feels good to relieve some tension from my stomach. I tap my glass. 'I don't know what's in this, but it's divine.'

We carry our drinks over to a table and sit close together. Thalia pats my arm.

'Ooh! Mrs Todgers mentioned you are an author now. Congratulations!'

A warm glow tingles my cheeks at her praise. 'Thank you. I'm not published yet, but yeah, I've been busy rewriting fairy tales for kids.'

Thalia rests her elbows on the table and fixes her gaze on me with an enthusiastic smile. 'Tell me more…'

I stroke the soft petals of the table decorations. 'My first story is about Cinderella – except this one is a spoilt brat and rude to everyone, and Prince Charming can't stand her.'

Thalia claps her hands and bursts out laughing. Unfortunately, with her mouth full of cocktail, she sprays the white drink across the table and down her uniform.

The barman rushes over with a pile of napkins and begins wiping up.

'I'm so sorry!' Thalia laughs, wiping herself down. I roar with laughter too, even more so at the shock of seeing Thalia's outburst than her snorting drink from her nose. She always seems reserved and professional. She reminds me of one of those movie characters who takes off her glasses, lets down her hair, and she's secretly a stunner.

'Tell me it's about Taylor.' She giggles.

'Well… yes, she was the inspiration.'

'Oh, I must read it! It's much more pleasant here now she's gone,' she whispers. 'Did you tell Mrs Todgers? She'll think it's a scream.'

Back behind the bar, the barman increases the volume of the background Christmas music. We've obviously been making too much of a commotion for this quiet little place – which sets us off laughing again. When our giggles die down, words are out of my mouth before I can stop them. 'How do you know when you can trust someone?' Admittedly, the question does seem quite random. I wish someone could just tell me, *Yes, you can trust him*.

Thalia looks up at the ceiling while she considers her answer. 'Hmmm, I think if someone is open with you and looks you in the eye when they talk. And if they seem kind and respectful to people. But mostly, I think you have to trust your intuition.'

I knew lovely, sweet Thalia was the right person to talk to. She's so sensible and calming to be around. My gut says I can trust him, but is that wishful thinking? I take a long drink. 'Is there anyone here that you don't trust?'

Thalia lowers her voice, although there's no one close to hear. 'Well, I know some of the staff get up to some questionable behaviours out of hours.'

'Anyone in particular?'

'I wouldn't like to say.'

Damn. She's too polite to give me any insider knowledge on Abbi.

I absentmindedly stroke the flower petals again. So, if I *did* go on the date... how do dates even work? What do we do? Or say? I feel awkward just thinking about it.

'If you had a date, how would you prepare? What would you wear? How much would you drink beforehand?' I daren't look up to see Thalia's reaction. This feels like the strangest interview ever.

She gasps. 'Do you have a date, Cally?' I take a quick peek at her face. Her eyes are twinkling. Excited-for-me twinkles though, not eager-to-hear-the-gossip twinkles. I wave her question away, accidentally pulling a few flowers out of their display. I hastily pile them back on top. Thalia doesn't notice. She's sitting up straight like she's in efficient work mode. 'First of all, where is the date?'

'Err... I don't know. Dinner, I guess.' I can't think what else we could do here.

'OK, if it was a special date, I would go to the spa and be pampered. I would get waxed in case, well, you know. And I would have my hair and make-up done.' There's an excited high pitch to her voice that makes my stomach clench with more nerves.

'And what would you wear?'

'If I didn't know where I was going... I would dress elegant but casual, you know what I mean?'

'Err... no?'

'Well, maybe a dress but with low heels.'

'Any other options?' I have no dresses. Or heels.

'Dress and high heels?'

I raise an eyebrow.

'No? OK. How about some black trousers with a slinky, low-cut top?'

I pout into my glass.

She leans forward and whispers, 'What do you have, Cally?'

'Jeans?'

'So it is you that has a date!' She squeals quietly. Damn. The flowers fall back down onto the table.

'Is it a date for the ball?'

I shake my head. 'Tonight.'

'Right. I'll make your appointments for the spa this afternoon and book Nanny Prim. And as we're both curvy' – she motions around her bust – 'I can lend you a top – I have the perfect thing. You'll blow him away.' She raises her eyebrows in a way to ask who the date's with. I fix the table decoration again, knowing she is too polite to ask outright.

'To date night!' She raises her glass for a toast. I tap my glass on hers, nerves firmly taking root.

'Ready, set, go…' Thalia stands and downs the rest of her drink. 'Give me five minutes.' Then she rushes back to reception with her new tasks.

I walk around to the private courtyard for an I'm-going-on-a-date-anxiety cigarette. It's no longer full of calming greenery, but the small area is still filled with twinkling lights and candles, and the snowy ground is untouched like it's my own quiet haven. Which means I don't have to hide my filthy habit like I'm a secret cannibal; I'm merely a social outcast.

As I light up, memories of this place come flooding back. The first time Jisung spoke to me and the embarrassment of him pointing out the chocolate smears. And our last time together in the summer – that heart-stopping kiss. The immense pain of having to walk away. Never did I ever imagine I'd be back here months later. Or that I'd be questioning his honesty.

And yet here we are now, about to go on a date. I don't remember ever going on a proper date before. Ben and I used to just hang out with friends when we first met. We went out, but never anything official or fancy. I've never had to order something unpronounceable from a menu or worry about which knife to use.

Leaving my marriage is a bit like waking up from a long, bad dream. In all those years, I never really lived at all. And if it wasn't for the whole Abbi thing, I would be so excited – a whole evening of him all to myself. Even if we just hang out as mates, maybe I could allow myself to feel a little bit excited?

I scurry back to meet Thalia at reception, feeling a little less guilty.

'It's all sorted. I'll walk over to the spa with you.' She has a huge grin, and I suddenly feel like we're keeping a big secret. If Diane found out, Jisung could get in big trouble. A jolt of fear strikes at the thought that I could even be sent home.

Once we're suitably clothed and outside, I ask, 'You didn't tell anyone, did you?'

She pats my shoulder. 'Your secret's safe with me,' she assures, her smile filled with mischief and a playful glint in her eye. 'I've booked you in for a full-body wax first.'

'Ugh! An hour of pain. Thanks!' I laugh.

'And then you'll have your hair and make-up done.' She smirks and whispers, 'He's a lucky man, whoever he is.'

'That's kind of you to say.'

'I'm not just being kind; it's the truth. Have you seen your seductive smile and those curves?'

My hands fly up to cover my mouth. My smile is seductive? Really? My cheeks flush.

'Cally, you're young, free, and single. He won't be able to resist you.'

I snort at her suggestion that I'm young. She has no idea how disconcerting it is when middle age creeps up on you without warning. Even reaching at the wrong angle to put on a sock can feel like I've fallen from a high-speed vehicle. But I guess she's right about the free and single part, which brings a big smile to my face. And activates all the laughter-line crinkles around my middle-aged eyes.

My insides are a jumble of nerves as another new member of staff greets me at the spa reception. I say goodbye to Thalia and follow the woman's overpowering cloud of perfume to my torture session.

Now I can speak to Abbi and find out the truth.

Except Abbi is not in the treatment room. It's Georgia – who can't give me the answers I need. Or maybe she can?

After our initial *it's so good to see you again* greetings, I assume the position on the warm, comfy bed ready for all the ouchies and intimate-area-torture silent screams. Hopefully silent anyway. Oh no, and hopefully no farts.

While she waxes my legs, I try to focus on the glorious fragrances of essential oils and the calming meditation music. But feeling zen is tricky when it feels like my skin is being ripped off.

'Last time I saw you, you were looking gorgeous and heading to the grand ball. How was it?' Georgia asks.

It was the magical night of my dreams until Prince Charming turned me down for a one-night stand, and I fell apart from the humiliation. But then he put me back together and it was beautiful, I want to respond, but go with, 'It was wonderful, thank you.'

The pain pauses temporarily while Georgia collects another wad of waxing cloths. My body is obviously more overgrown and gorilla-like than she expected.

'There were three of you helping me get ready that day – poor you, having to cope with me by yourself today!'

'I could always call Daisy for emergency backup.' We both giggle. 'But we're a person down today. Abbi's off with an awful cold. Staff are dropping like flies. It's a nightmare at this time of year.'

Typical! After all my nerves today, it turns out I couldn't have spoken to Abbi anyway. Nonetheless, to take my mind off the pain, suffering, and embarrassment Georgia inflicts with her lady gardening, I seize my opportunity.

'So, Abbi said she has a new man!'

'Yeah, tall, dark, and handsome, apparently.'

'You haven't met him?' My words are accompanied by a ripping sound and end as a high-pitched squeak.

Georgia spreads a new patch of hot wax on my intimate areas. 'No, she's being quite secretive.'

'Has she been seeing him for long?' I grit my teeth in preparation for the next burn of my flesh.

Georgia gives one final yank, and then it feels as though she's pricking me with pins as she dabs the cloth over small spots of wax that remain. 'I don't think so.'

Her news brings a little relief, as does the end of my gruelling waxing session. Georgia smothers me with a delicious-smelling cooling lotion before wrapping me in soft towels to recover.

***

After some much-needed recuperation, Daisy comes into the room offering a chilled glass of champagne. I sit up, in an awkward state of undress, and we share a hug. During our *long time no see* greetings, she helps me to my feet and wraps me in a warm dressing gown.

'I'm so sorry, Cally. I have some bad news.' Daisy dips her head, and mine springs up in panic. Before my mind has time to conjure up any potential disasters, she says, 'Abbi's off sick today and we've had a difficult time trying to cover for her, and because yours was a last-minute booking…'

'Oh my goodness, don't worry.' I put my hand on her arm and she looks at me with *sorry I pooed in your shoe* puppy-dog eyes.

'Honestly, it's no problem at all.'

The look of guilt on her face visibly fades, and she raises a timid smile. 'But if it's any good for you, I can come to your room and do your make-up when I finish here at six o'clock?'

'Oh, Daisy, that is so kind of you.' I smile and give her a hug. 'That would be perfect timing for me. It means I can join Lexi for the Christmas lights event first, without your hard work getting spoiled outside.'

Daisy beams. 'You'll love it! But it's about to begin, so you'll need to hurry.'

***

I make a quick dash back to our hotel room to collect our named baubles that Lexi unwrapped from under our tree, then rush back outside to find her. In the dark, I follow the hum of music and round a corner just in time to catch the final colourful flickers of the Christmas tree lights switching on. The gigantic tree towers above a large crowd, casting a brilliant glow over the cheering revellers.

The air is thick with excitement, the buzz of conversation and laughter mingling with the sweet sound of children singing Christmas carols.

I am infused with the festive energy as I approach and make my way through to the front where the children are. Lexi is standing with her new friends beside the beautifully lit tree, singing her heart out. The sight makes my breath shudder, and a lump forms in my throat. It's like being moved to tears at the happy ending of a Christmas movie. When their carol ends, I wave to get her attention and she comes running over.

'Mum! I'm so glad you came.' She throws her arms around me and I'm so thankful to be here with her. We snuggle up together, both joining in with the rest of the carols while I try to hide the occasional happy teardrop. A mum crying at a Christmas carol would not be good for Lexi's street cred. Between songs, I get just enough time to ask about her afternoon.

'It was so much fun! I got a prize! It was a snow fairy for the top of the Christmas tree in our bedroom. And they told stories and we acted out the parts, and then the Ice Queen came and tried to catch us, and then we went snow-fairy dancing in the snow!'

'Aww, it sounds amazing. Did Nanny P come to find you?'

'No, Prince Charming looked after me.'

'Oh! Is he here then?' I ask, looking around.

She points to the side of the tree. 'He's over there.'

And there he is, smiling over at us, his handsome face glowing different colours from the tree lights. My stupid stomach flips. We hold each other's gaze, probably far too noticeably if anyone had been watching. I look down, the hurt of reality dampening my hopeful heart. What if Abbi was watching? What if I looked up and she was there, draped all over him, claiming him? What if he's lying to me? I could be about to go on a date with a liar and a cheat.

I'm so confused. I wish the universe would give me a sign, the all-clear, the go-ahead. But not with green or red lights, because they keep flashing on the tree anyway. I watch his smiling face across the tree, wanting so badly to let myself feel, but my feet stay frozen in doubt.

One of the guys in orange invites all the children to hang their baubles on the tree. I hand Lexi her ornament, and just as she's about to run forward, Prince Charming scoops her up and settles her onto his broad shoulders. She squeals as he dashes to the tree to find the perfect spot for her bauble. When they turn back around, her delighted glow makes the hairs on my arms stand on end, even underneath all my layers. Another feel-good movie moment – I hope the photographers are around to capture her smile.

Then the grown-ups are invited to hang their baubles. Lexi is lowered while the rush of adults clears, and Jisung and I step forward. But suddenly, a mischievous head pops up between my legs, and before I can react, I'm hoisted into the air, perched precariously on his shoulders. I unleash loud, adult-sized squeals, fearing for my life, much to the amusement of everyone near. I grab hold of his head, and my hands tangle in his hair, grasp his face, under his chin, desperately trying to stay balanced. Still squealing, heart racing, I grip the flimsy branches of the tree, its needles prickling my hands while I place my bauble next to Lexi's. I am well aware I am Calamity Cally, and visions of toppling the tree onto us don't leave my worries until my feet are firmly back on the ground.

Still laughing, Jisung positions his Prince Charming bauble just below ours. His smile makes my heart skip, bringing back memories of our time together this summer. 'Hey, Lexi.' Jisung takes her hand and points up. 'See how our baubles are hanging in a triangle shape?'

Lexi slips her hand in mine as they gaze up at the tree, while I watch the wonder on Lexi's face illuminated by the flickering lights.

'They're all connected together like they're holding hands.' The warmth in his voice chips away at my icy doubts. Being near him like this, it just feels right. Could this really be the Christmas miracle I hoped for but didn't dare fully imagine? He then takes hold of my hand, his gaze moving between Lexi and me.

'Just like the three of us are all close and holding hands. Isn't that cool?'

A smile spreads across Lexi's face, wide and radiant, and even though I'm slightly jealous that she lets him get away with saying 'cool' without an eye roll, my heart bursts for her. And a little bit for me too. It's hard to ignore that this whole experience could well be the sign I was looking for, and it's certainly made a little girl (and her mum) feel very special.

The merriment continues as the mulled wine is passed around and we all sing 'O Christmas Tree'. My Ben-and-Abbi bah-humbugs have been pushed aside for now, and I couldn't feel more festive if I was wrapped in tinsel with a star stuck on my head. We are so lucky to be here; I must work extra hard tomorrow.

The Christmas lights show begins and thousands of twinkling lights burst to life all around us, bathing the crowd in ever-changing kaleidoscopes of colour dancing along with the music. The atmosphere is electric; everyone is filled with the season's cheer, swaying and clapping along as we all watch in awe. And as more mulled wine flows, the dancing and singing becomes more lively and the joyful laughter is contagious. We're part of a festive community, with families celebrating around our own personalised Christmas tree.

I sneak glances at Jisung's upturned face, his child-like wonder making him even more handsome. Lexi and I join hands with him, connecting the three of us as we lose ourselves in the magical lights. For these few minutes, all my worries fade away. And for a moment, it feels like we're a little family of three. A happy little family. And it feels simply perfect. But I quickly wipe my mind clean of dreams and expectations – they only lead to bitter disappointment.

Nearing six o'clock, guests begin to drift off in search of dinner and I hear a whisper in my ear: 'Meet you in the lobby at seven.' I nod, a nervous flutter in my chest.

'Time for us to find Nanny P, my darling. You must be starving.'

***

At twenty minutes to seven, Daisy has just finished my hair and make-up. Nothing over the top, just elegant and casual. I still have no real idea what this means, but Daisy understood the brief. Even though she seemed to use hundreds of products, I look as if I have fresh, natural skin with a touch of healthy colour to my cheeks and soft smoky eyes. She gives me a final once-over. 'Nope, it's not quite right.' She shakes her head. 'We need some finishing flourishes.'

'Whatever you think is best. I trust you.'

A few minutes later, Daisy sings, 'Ta-dah! That's better. Now we have sultry glamour-puss eyes,' she says to my reflection in the mirror. 'Sexy black winged eyeliner and long flirty eyelashes. *Prrrrr!* And... look at those luscious pouty lips. Mwah! You could snog all night and this won't rub off.'

I hardly recognise myself, and I can't help but flutter my eyelashes and make pouty faces in the mirror, making us both giggle.

'Daisy, I look... fabulous!' I try out some more over-the-top flirtatious poses in the mirror, which I would never dream of doing anywhere in real life. Daisy joins in too.

'What are you up to this evening, anyway?'

I had managed to get away without disclosing the date to Daisy, or mentioning any reason, in fact, for today's urgent pampering. 'I have a hot date.' I laugh as though it's the most preposterous joke while inwardly quaking as time pushes on.

Daisy helps me into Thalia's silky cream top. 'You know you can't wear a bra with this top?' she says, trying to align the straps.

'What? I can't go on a date bra-less. Not with these great bazoomas!'

Daisy gasps and her mouth falls open. She stares at me. I stare back at her, realising my error. I've broken my own secret. As expected, she fires questions, wanting to hear *everything*.

'I don't have time to explain, Daisy!' I fluster. 'I'll tell you how it all goes later?'

'Of course, Little Miss Secretive.' She giggles.

'And I have to wear a bra, sorry.'

I needn't have worried. Daisy's like a pampering whirlwind. In no time, I'm dressed, spritzed, and glossed, and ready to go.

While Daisy packs away, I pace around the room and then examine myself in front of the mirror again. 'I can't go early and stand around. What if I get stood up?'

Yep, nerves have well and truly kicked in. 'Daisy, you, me, bar, now!'

We both laugh, and I grab my hoodie, just in case, as we head to the bar.

***

Once we've ordered our champagne, I look down and realise I'm still wearing my comfy slippers. Daisy follows my eyes down. 'Well, you did say casual…'

'I guess I did.' I laugh, deliriously high on adrenaline. 'Ooh Daisy, I meant to ask, what's going on with Abbi's new man?'

'Hmmm, I don't know,' she says suspiciously, her eyes almost closed. 'It's odd we haven't met him or even seen him, don't you think?' Our champagne arrives. I glance at the clock and down nearly all of mine in one gulp.

'Strictly between you and me' – she raises her eyebrows and I nod – 'I wonder if she's living in delulu land?'

'Err… where?'

'The land of delusions,' she says slowly and quietly. Then she whispers behind her hand, 'It wouldn't be the first time.'

My eyebrows shoot up and I give her a big kiss on the cheek. 'Daisy, I love you. Thank you for everything. I have to run.' I leave the bar with a Lexi-sized beaming smile.

WEDNESDAY

Mushroom House

I pop into the bathroom to wipe away the pools of sweat from my armpits and use the rest of the complimentary can of spray deodorant. My stomach churns with nerves or excitement or hunger. I wish I'd asked where we were going. It feels awkward meeting for a date wearing a strappy silk top with slippers. I throw on my hoodie in case of any potential sweat patches. Taking one last look in the mirror, I feel slightly more confident with what I see, and for old time's sake, I bite my top lip in a sexy Frankenstein way. Giggling at my reflection, I step out into the lobby.

Jisung is there. My breath catches in my throat as I'm hit with a rush of relief and nerves, my heart racing wildly. Please, gods of deodorant, don't fail me now. He stands facing the door wearing his full outdoor kit, and as I take a slow step towards him, I remember we both said our ideal dates would be going for a walk. My shoulders relax down from my ears – no fancy restaurants, no staring guests or nosy staff – much less pressure. I stop at the cloakroom to swap my slippers for boots and get my coat. *Now* I'm ready.

I quietly approach him from behind and lean in to whisper in his ear, 'Meet you outside.' With that, I step outside into the chilly air and wait at the bottom of the staircase. A few moments later, Jisung emerges and jokingly calls out far too loudly, 'Are you ashamed of being seen with me?'

I glance around to check nobody has overheard, and he runs down the stairs with a big grin. I cross my arms over my chest and smirk. 'Where's my helicopter?'

He jumps down the last steps, grabs me, and twirls me around, laughing, 'Where's your dog?'

We link arms and begin walking in comfortable silence, veering around the back of the hotel and away from any prying eyes. Then he stops. He turns to face me and drapes his arms loosely around my shoulders. My arms instinctively sneak around his waist.

'Let me look at you.' He lets out a playful sigh. I look up into his beautiful face, fighting back the swooning hearts in my eyes.

His eyes narrow. 'Are you teasing me?'

I jerk my head back. 'Huh?'

'Looking so foxy for me tonight.' He bites his lip, and I lower my head with a bashful chuckle.

'Still as cute as ever.'

I link my arm through his again, tugging him forward. He grins and says, 'Let's go and find our mushroom house in the woods.'

I glance at his side profile. I can't believe he remembers these little things we spoke about in the summer.

'Thank you for looking after Lexi today; she had great fun.' I know I'm putting off what I really want to say.

'It was my pleasure. She's a great kid, fun to be around.'

'She must really like you to choose you instead of Nanny P.' We both laugh, and I glance around at him again. Even in this dim light I notice signs of fatigue etched on his features and the shadows under his eyes. I hug his arm, and he takes my hand, pulling it inside his pocket. I sigh. It has to be said.

'Jisung, I have to know. I can work with the truth, but I just need to know.'

His forehead wrinkles. 'Is this still about Abbi?'

I stop still, frustration mounting. 'Yes, it's still about Abbi!'

He turns to face me and strokes my cheek. Looking directly into my eyes, he says firmly but gently, 'I told you there is nothing going on with Abbi.'

I look down. I don't want to have this conversation any more than he does.

'I want to believe you, but I saw her fling herself at you and go to kiss you... I have to protect myself from getting hurt even more.'

He puts his hand on the back of my head and kisses my forehead, resting his head against mine for a long moment.

'OK, I'll tell you the whole truth, but promise me you'll hear me out until the end.'

I freeze. Now I'm scared to hear the truth, but I know it's the only way. I cough, unable to speak.

'Do you promise, Cally?'

I nod. He gently pulls up my chin to look into my eyes, making it feel even more difficult to prepare myself for whatever he's about to reveal.

He slowly releases a drawn-out sigh. 'You are not someone who is easy to forget, Cally Jackson.

You bloomed roses in my heart where there were only thorns.'

I suck in a sharp breath. Those are not words I ever thought I would hear. I want to melt into his arms, but I know there's more to come. There's sadness in his eyes.

'When you left, my heart was broken. I was lost – for a long time.' He swallows and his voice quietens. 'I didn't know if you would ever come back to me, or whether you would stay with your husband.'

'I –'

He puts his finger to my lips. 'Hear me out, please.'

I kiss his finger. My eyes pop open wide, and he grins. The surprise breaks the tension for a moment.

'I knew I couldn't contact you. It had to be your decision. And in all honesty, it made me realise how lonely I felt here, without my friends and family.' He looks away and runs his hand through his hair. 'Can we walk? This is hard.'

He reaches out to me, and I squeeze his hand as a friend caring for a friend. Even if he is about to tear my heart to shreds. He leads us onto a new path where the trees cast gnarly shadows over the snow. I have no idea where we're going.

'I thought about going back to Korea. I even asked my manager to put me forward for jobs back home.' He pauses and takes a deep breath, as if to inhale some courage. 'So when Abbi began flirting with me, I realised I missed having someone to care about me.' He chokes out his words. I choke back tears. He sighs again. I can hear how difficult this is to talk about. My heart is thumping wildly. I don't want to hear what's coming next.

'But Abbi wasn't you. I didn't have a connection with her. And it made me so sad because I didn't know if I would ever see you again.' He squeezes my hand tightly.

'You are right. She did throw herself at me, a few times, but each time I brushed her off.' He stops to face me. 'Nothing happened between us. Please believe me.'

I put my hands on his cold cheeks, holding his gaze as the last of my doubts and fear melt away, and anything seems possible between us again.

His dark eyes search mine for a reaction, and in them I see everything – affection, regret, hope, desire. My fingers trail down to his mouth, and I lean in close, buoyed by the feel of his breath against my skin once more.

'And then I came back to you, but I thought I was too late,' I whisper with a frown. My lips find his, and I kiss him tenderly, feeling as though I've finally come home.

The tension that's built between us over months of longing seems to dissipate all at once. I sigh into his embrace, 'I'm sorry I pushed you away, and for hurting you too. I wish we had talked all this through straight away. Then I wouldn't have missed precious time with you.'

He catches my mouth in another gentle kiss, sending all remaining worries fleeing from my mind. 'You're here now – that's all that matters.' He takes my hand and kisses my palm. 'So you're not still angry?'

'What, because you have feelings?' I give him the biggest, longest hug. 'I jumped to conclusions and didn't listen. I'm so sorry.' I caused my own pain and anguish, mostly. And now I want to make up for every lost second.

I look up and down the path, but I don't recognise where we are in the dark – there's just more trees and more snow. 'Can we go somewhere inside so I can hug you without all these layers of padding?' I hold out my puffed-up arms.

He puts his arm around my shoulder and kisses the top of my head. 'We're nearly there.'

I look up at him with a grin. 'You know we don't really have a mushroom house?'

He squeezes my shoulders, pulling me close to him as we continue walking. 'You make me laugh.'

'Err... laugh with me or at me?'

'A bit of both.' The pair of us laugh, and I slip my arm around him. This is how it should have been all week.

'Oh, did you get your replacement coat?'

'I did, and the handkerchief with your sweet message. Thank you.' He squeezes me again.

'I took your coat home accidentally. But I used it as a pillow every night. I never forgot you.'

'I left my heart in the pocket for you.' How could I not adore this man when he says such things? He stops walking and hugs me. 'We're here.'

I look around. It doesn't seem like we're anywhere. 'Umm... where?'

'Our date.'

Jisung pulls aside a branch and waves for me to go under. Unfortunately, my cat-eye make-up doesn't give me the enhanced feline night vision to see anything apart from trees, and I grab on to Jisung's arm. But as we walk a little further into the wooded wilderness, there are lights ahead. And what appears to be a wooden house with a long, sloping roof.

'What is this place?'

'I wanted to take you on a steamy Korean date, but it was a bit hard at the resort.'

I laugh. 'What kind of steamy date?'

'This was the closest thing I could find to a bathhouse. There's no sauna though. I'm sorry.'

'I don't even know what a bathhouse is, but anywhere we can be together is perfect.'

Around the back of this secluded chalet, a soft and inviting glow emanates from the strings of fairy lights delicately draped across a covered veranda. On the far side of the cabin, a domed conservatory catches my eye. Jisung takes hold of my hand and twirls me around, allowing me to take in the breathtaking view. His arms encircle me, and he rests his head gently on my shoulder.

Together, we stand, gazing out over the vast slopes of pristine snow, their iridescent sheen illuminated by the soft glow of the moonlight. The clear night sky stretches wide above, offering a perfect view of countless stars shining brightly against the inky blackness.

I turn back to face Jisung, and overwhelmed with gratitude, I throw my arms around him. 'Thank you for bringing me to such a magical place.'

'It's not a mushroom house, but I hope you like it.' He takes my hand. 'Let's go in.'

We follow the short path where the snow has been cleared and climb the chalet steps, passing a hot tub on the wooden veranda. Inside is like a cosy little cottage – open-plan, with soft lighting and a large couch opposite a roaring fire. We hang up our coats and step into the comfy slippers waiting beneath the coat stand. Jisung opens the bottle of champagne that has been left for us on a small table and pours us each a glass.

'This place is so romantic.' I wince at my choice of words. It's not part of my usual vocabulary and feels uncomfortable to use. I need to pinch myself awake. I can't believe I'm here on a date, with this incredible man, in this beautiful place. Jisung hands me my champagne, which I immediately drain, noticing the glass trembling in my fingers. I quickly put it down and ruffle the back of my hair. I can feel him looking at me with my nerves on display.

'Make yourself at home. This place is ours for the evening.' He puts his arm around my shoulder and pulls me closer. 'Relax, it's just us.'

I point to a plate of chocolate-coated strawberries with a nervous grin. 'May I?'

He takes one, lifts it to my mouth, and feeds me with a cheeky glint in his eye. Damn! Why is everything so ultra-romantic, and why does it make me want to explode from nervous energy?

I take a step back and stumble as my foot leaves my slipper behind, which really doesn't help when I'm trying to steady my breathing. I take hold of Jisung's hands but can't quite make eye contact. 'I know this is a date… but… I need you to be my friend too.' I look down to pause.

'We can take things as slow as you want to, Cally. I don't want to cause any burden to you.'

I squeeze his hands, still unable to meet his gaze. 'This is all new and strange for me. I was married for a long time. I don't know how to go on a date. I'm… scared.'

He pulls me to him and gives me a big bear hug. 'I've got you.' He holds me tight and I wrap my arms around his back. It's a protective hug, comforting, calming. A hug in this moment, not filled with hopes or dreams or fears – it's just the two of us, open and vulnerable, here and now.

'I've wanted this for so long,' he whispers, his warm breath against my temple. His lips brush across my forehead. I could stay like this forever, my head on his chest, my hands running over his muscular back.

I relax into his body, relieved the confusion is over. 'I thought you didn't want me.' The words fall out of my lips like they're releasing the strain of the past few days, months.

He pulls back slightly, tilting his head and gazing into my eyes with a gentle stare that penetrates and soothes my soul. After a long moment, he breathes out, 'May I kiss you?'

I stretch my head up and stand on tiptoes; he leans down, and our lips meet. Our kiss is soft and slow, healing the pain we have both been through.

When we eventually come up for air, he brings a fresh energy to our conversation. 'Bathhouses are where we go to relax and have fun – families, couples, friends. First we shower and scrub down, then go into the hot and cold baths. Hmm, usually men and women have separate areas, but here we will share the hot tub, if that is OK? Then we all rest together in the sauna. I will take you to my favourite *jimjilbang* one day.'

He gives me a sparkling smile, looking so proud that he's arranged to share this with me. I stare at him, gripping my sleeves over my hands to feel the reassurance of clothing. 'Sorry, what? We're going to be naked? Now?'

'No! We will wear swimming costumes here.'

'On a date? Daisy already did my make-up.'

His eyes sweep up and down my body. 'And you look beautiful.' He kisses my cheek.

I shake my head. First I'm nervous, and then I have to take my clothes off. I need alcohol stat. I refill my glass. 'I'm going to need a lot of these.' I raise my glass with a nervous giggle.

His face drops. 'You don't like it? We can stay indoors by the fire if you prefer?'

I put my hand on his arm. 'No, it's very thoughtful, thank you.' Well, it's different to a pint at the local pub, I suppose. He's seen me in a bikini before and has still invited me here, so the sight of my body shouldn't come as a shock. What the hell – you only live once!

He gestures to a basket on the table. 'Help yourself. I'm going to jump in the shower first... unless you want to join me?' he jests, wiggling his eyebrows and making me giggle.

'Shower.' I nod. This is really happening. I don't know why I'm surprised. This could only happen to me! Time for Badass Cally to come out to play.

'It's just through there.' He points to the side of the cabin. It's only then I properly take notice of the interior. There's a glass door to the conservatory through which I can see a sign saying *Bathroom*, where Jisung is now heading.

I take the picnic basket over to the couch and rest back against the cushions, feeling both apprehensive and blown away by all of the evening's events. Surely I'll wake up from this bizarre dream soon. But that kiss… just thinking of it sends me into a swoony head spin.

It's a bit too toasty sitting near the fire, so I take off my hoodie and, feeling like my cheeks are getting sunburned, shield my face with my hand. I spy another bottle of champagne poking out of the basket. I definitely don't feel like eating now, but I do need a boost of courage.

I head over to refill my glass again. Hmm. If I'm going to be practically naked, then so is… Jisung emerges from the bathroom.

'Cally, I'm so sorry. The housekeepers have forgotten to restock the towels.' He laughs awkwardly. 'There's only this size.' I don't know where to look. His skin is wet and glistening, hair dripping into his eyes, and he's only wearing his boxer shorts, using the small towel to cover his privates. I daren't try to only look him in the eye, so I hold out his glass while looking straight outside.

He walks over, puts the glass back down, and stands behind me. 'Mmmm, that top is too much. You're irresistible.' He kisses my neck and puts his hands on my silky waist, which I guess means his towel has dropped to the floor. I can't breathe. He covers my shoulders with feathery kisses that send tingles down my spine. I lean my head back, enjoying every single one. 'Your turn in the shower. I'll meet you in the hot tub.'

'But… the towels! And swimming costume!' I panic.

'I think there is something in the cupboard you can wear, but you don't need to worry. There's only me here.' He kisses my neck and then walks past me to go outside. His bottom is impossible to resist, and I give it a good slap.

'That's it!' He turns on me as if to retaliate. I squeal and run.

***

In the bathroom, I first check the supplies cupboard. One tiny towel, no bigger than a tea towel. I take out two pieces of string, each threaded with two tiny triangles of material. I'm already mortified. I undress, attempt to tie the strings around my body and adjust the positions of the triangles, but they may as well not even be there for the coverage they provide. I jump under the shower. Maybe they're like those magic face cloths that expand in water? But no such luck. Surely I don't need to get my hair wet? I don't plan on any underwater hot-tub diving. I quickly wash, scrubbing off my layer of deodorant, and continue to adjust the triangles. It's hopeless. They are barely wide enough to cover my nipples. Thank goodness for Georgia's torturous lady gardening earlier. It's OK for Jisung and his model-perfect body. So do I use the towel to cover my top or bottom half? This is taking first-date jitters to a whole new level.

On my way out of the warmth and privacy of the cabin, I grab the champagne and glasses. I end up looking like I'm working as a waitress in the most dubious home movie. I step outside to find Jisung isn't even there. The hot tub is steaming, and before my nipples freeze off, I put down my wares and climb in. I sink into the blissful warm water.

Ahh, now this really is the life. As far as dates go, things could always be worse. My eyes flick up to the sky. Just to let you know, Universe, that was not an invitation. No bubble bath or drowning, pretty please. Where is my date anyway?

'Jisung?'

'I'm down here!'

I swish through the water and look over the side of the veranda. 'What the hell?' He's in a hole in the snowy ground full of icy water. 'Come out of there. You'll die!' My voice carries out to the dark trees surrounding our garden.

'This is a natural polar bear plunge pool. It's fine!'

'No it's not! Come out now!'

'If you say so.' He laughs and begins to climb up the ladder to ground level. I squeak and cover my eyes as if I've never seen a man only in boxers before. However, I've never seen *that* kind of man in boxers before – one who's so sizzling hot, it's no wonder he doesn't feel the cold. And I couldn't help but notice… I'm sure I've heard before that the cold makes *things* shrink? But if that was its shrunken state, *Oh. My. Goodness!*

I keep my eyes covered until I hear him splash into the hot tub beside me. I gasp when I open my eyes, which I try to cover with a cough. I can't believe this gorgeous almost-naked man is sitting so close to me. I hold my arms around me to cover the triangles. 'You're crazy! Don't do that again. You'll freeze to death!'

'I go in cold pools all the time back home. It's good for you.' He laughs at me. 'And anyway, don't you do *that*!'

'What?'

'Making me want to kiss you.'

I laugh back at him. 'I didn't do anything!'

'You're doing it again!'

'Such a smooth talker.'

'I'm serious!' He lifts his arms out of the water and gestures. 'Come to me.'

'No, I'm embarrassed by this bikini. There's nothing to it.' I sink lower under the bubbling water.

'Even better.' He wiggles his eyebrows and we both laugh. He passes my glass and we sit, drink, and relax. Or at least, as much as I can relax when all I want to do is run my fingers over that bare chest.

Jisung sees my glass is empty and goes to pour more champagne, but there's only a drip left in the bottle.

'Uh oh! Someone will have to get the other bottle from inside.' I smirk. 'I promise I won't look.'

He laughs. 'No, no, no... I want to see you in that bikini!'

'Noooo!' I know my cheeks have gone bright red.

'Rock, paper, scissors?' he suggests, still laughing. I nod.

'One, two, three.' We both splash a hand out of the water. His fist does rock, but I do paper.

'Ha! I win!' I cover my eyes with my hand, clearly peeping through my fingers as he lifts himself out of the water. But the man is not shy. He must hear me gasp, and I cover my face with both hands. Sorry, Daisy; the make-up's ruined, but I guarantee you would have done the same if you were faced with the... *Ji-conda*.

Seconds later, he comes out with the bottle and plate of strawberries. I don't cover my eyes this time. I want to see his body in its full glory. And my goodness, it is glorious. He sits next to me and opens the champagne, then reaches for a strawberry and teases me with it, bringing it close to my lips and then pulling it away. After three teases, I grab his hand and take a bite. He squidges the whole thing into my mouth, strawberry juice squished all over my face, and we laugh like mischievous children. We drink more and rest back in the bubbles. I suddenly remember my manners. 'Would you like a strawberry?'

'Hmm, no thank you. My appetite has suddenly changed.' He winks at me, making us laugh again. His playful humour puts me at ease. This may be the strangest date in history, but it's the most fun I've had in forever. My life has felt stale and heavy for so long, I had forgotten how to enjoy myself. This man is a breath of fresh air and when we're together, I feel alive. He reminds me I am a woman as well as a mum.

I sit up, flustered. 'What time is it?'

'If you're worried about getting back for Lexi, I hope you don't mind but I spoke to Nanny P earlier… she's happy to set up a camp bed and stay with Lexi for the night.'

With a sharp intake of breath, I turn to face Jisung. 'So she knows we're out together?'

'Hmm.' He nods. 'Is that not OK?'

'What if she says something? We could both get in trouble.'

'She won't say anything, and don't worry, we won't get into trouble.' He puts his arm around my shoulder. 'We can be back early before Lexi wakes up.'

'But where would we sleep?'

He points to the domed conservatory. 'It's a bedroom with a glass roof so we can watch the sun rise. But we don't have to… I can sleep on the couch… there's no pressure. What do you say?'

I lean in and kiss him, and relax, staying snuggled under his arm. He's thought of everything.

'There is just one more thing…'

I sit back up and look at him.

'When do I get to see this bikini?' He laughs and grabs me, tickling my sides. I squeal and splash him until he holds me in a tight cuddle.

Nestled in his arms, I feel secure, but my heart starts to race. Jisung is a gentleman, and when he says there's no pressure, I think that means he's not going to make the first move. And I want more – I want a physical connection. Which means it's down to me. I've had enough champagne to feel a little more confident, but am I brave enough to go for what I want? I think he's given signs that he wants me, but can I get over the fear that he might reject me again?

I take a deep breath. It's time to be Badass Cally. Another deep breath and I think I'm ready. And to be perfectly honest, I can't keep my hands off him any longer. I take a last deep breath and stand up. Screw the string bikini.

I rise from the water. My shyness immediately melts away under the heat of Jisung's penetrating gaze. His eyes widen, mouth falling open at the sight of my triangles on display.

For a second, he simply stares, drinking in every inch as I stand laid almost-bare before him. A low groan escapes him. 'You're exquisite,' he rasps.

In seconds he's beside me, hands tracing reverent paths along my curves. I shiver, though not from cold. He sees me as I've longed to be seen – desirable, wanted. His touch ignites a fire in my veins, banishing the last of my self-consciousness.

'God, Cally.' His voice is rough with need. 'The things you make me want to do…' He lifts me onto his lap, nibbling a path along my neck. I sigh, losing myself in the eager exploration of his hands, his mouth, the fervent kisses punctuated by gasps and moans of pleasure.

He traces his finger down the string to my chest. He stops at the top of the triangle. 'May I keep going?'

'Yes, please,' I murmur into his lips.

***

After a long while of pent-up passion, we drip our way to the conservatory bedroom. We switch on the lamps, and on top of the small dresser is a tall pile of towels and robes, t-shirts, and shorts, which never made it to the bathroom. Laughing, we dry ourselves off and snuggle into the bed. Lying with my head on his chest, we look up through the glass ceiling, gazing at the stars.

For a short time, at least. Until he turns to me with a twinkle in his eye. And finally, I get to devour him…

THURSDAY

Reality Calls

Waking up with the light of the rising sun streaming through the glass dome, cuddling the man of my dreams, is more than worth the grogginess from having very little sleep. If only I could start every day like this, even if it is ridiculous o'clock. I carefully untangle my limbs from his and hobble my way to the shower.

I've got a big day today with so much work to do. The review should have been my focus this week; now somehow I'll need to concentrate and earn our stay.

Did I learn nothing from the stress I caused myself last time by leaving it all until the last minute? No, no I did not.

But right now I have to get back before Lexi wakes up so I can avoid a barrage of awkward questions. Thankfully, my mind and body are exhausted; otherwise, I would be jumping and clicking my heels together all the way back to the hotel, screaming, *I've just had the best night of my entire life!*

I shower and get dressed back into yesterday's clothes. When I return to the bedroom, my skin tingles as I look down at this incredible man sleeping peacefully. How I long to climb back in the bed and snuggle up with him.

In the light of day, I can see an alarm clock on the dresser. I set the alarm for a more reasonable hour and softly kiss his forehead goodbye. I feel awful for creeping away, leaving him and the mess behind.

A note! I can leave him a note for when he wakes up. I search around the cabin, looking for a pen, but find nothing. I've got no lipstick or eyeliner with me. Shampoo? No, too weird. I check in the picnic basket… chocolate fudge cake it will have to be. And a napkin. I stick my finger in the fudge, draw a heart as best I can, and leave it on my pillow.

As I trace my steps in reverse up the snowy path, my body hums from the memory of Jisung's touch, and I'm overwhelmed by the euphoria of finally connecting so completely.

After the barren emotional intimacy of my marriage, I never dreamed I'd allow myself to be vulnerable again, trusting another with not just my body but my battered heart. But Jisung saw past my fears. And in his arms, I remembered the woman I used to be and could be again.

I duck under a branch, then with a surreptitious glance around and head down, I begin the morning-after *walk of shame* back to the hotel.

***

After a lovely breakfast chatting with Lexi about her *penguins on ice* skating escapades yesterday evening, she heads off for a morning of singing and dancing and I go to Diane's office. I'm quietly relieved when she's not there, and instead, I take Shana with me for some much-needed caffeine.

We head to an uncrowded indoor café, and I pour myself a coffee from the buffet. Eyes propped open with imaginary matchsticks, I sit with coffee cup in hand and a smile fixed in place. Shana has her laptop at the ready. 'Have you had a chance to think about any improvements to the guest experience?'

Ah. So that was what Diane asked me to do. 'Well, I'd like to run some thoughts by you before I start.' Damn, I didn't mean to say start. Now she'll know I haven't done anything yet.

I think back to our first visit in the summer. 'I've been thinking about the brochure, and I think we should cut the marketing speak altogether and go for a more intimate touch to highlight the guests' experiences and show the resort's personalised service.'

My throat has already dried out. This morning's not going to happen without more coffee. Shana taps away on her keyboard. Diane was right; she is efficient. I could do with my own Shana.

'I expect the majority of guests know what to expect of an exclusive resort, so I don't think we need lists of facilities and services. Instead we should have guest testimonials, including those of children. After all, families will be coming here primarily for the children's entertainment rather than an adults-only resort.' I wonder if she can tell I'm making this up as I go along? A server walks past and I attract her attention – I need a sugar fix.

'Good morning, ladies. What can I get for you?' Her voice is high-pitched and she seems very jolly. Oh yeah, it's almost Christmas.

'Hello, please could I have two of your largest, strongest coffees with chocolate fudge cake and a toffee knickerbocker glory with hidden vitamins please?'

Shana reaches out for my arm and whispers, 'Oh, I only wanted a glass of water, Cally.'

'And a glass of water, please?'

'Coming right up.'

I turn back to Shana, who is staring at me but too polite to question my order.

'Where was I?'

'Children's testimonials,' Shana confirms.

'Yes, and photographs… I think we need photos that show the guests enjoying the facilities, still keeping some of the resort's features hidden for them to discover. But we should mention they have surprises in store.' Come on, brain, think!

'I suggest we reconsider the no-cameras rule so guests can advertise for us on their social media. I'd like to see some professional photographer points around the resort, with gorgeous backdrops where guests can interact and pose with the cast of characters. We can send the photos electronically and encourage guests to upload them to Instagram with resort hashtags.' I'm well outside my remit now, whatever my remit actually is, but this is what my brain is chucking out.

'I think we need to highlight both the family fun entertainment as well as the nanny service and relaxation facilities for parents. And have some activities for solo parents, even if it's just an area to snuggle up for some frivolous fireside reading. And drinks. And snacks.' OK, I'm on a roll.

'We should introduce a newsletter for the children so they can stay in touch with their favourite characters; there's no harm in a bit of pester power to encourage re-booking. We should individualise the newsletters so it's like a club – kids love belonging to clubs.'

My coffee and sugar arrives, but I'm so focused that I hardly notice.

'And I suggest the characters provide the information about the family entertainment, and we could add lines of merchandise for each of them. In fact,' my brain cells whir into overdrive, and I wag my finger excitedly at my genius, 'I should write books about the individual characters and the adventures they get up to in the resort! Oh, and the website needs updating with video testimonials and clips of the entertainment. We need to install a booth where guests can record their reviews while they're here, ready to post on social media after their holidays.'

I finally pause for some delicious toffee goodness. 'I'm also thinking,' I say with my mouth full of cream, but there's no time to lose, 'themed weekend stays for children and for adults, like a weekend stage school and writers' retreats, yoga, art – things that could use the setting here for inspiration.' I drain my coffee; I need more caffeine power. 'And weekend weddings! We have such magical settings here for outdoor weddings. And filming! During quieter times, we could hire out parts of the grounds as movie sets and for photoshoots.' I'm so far from my brief now, I've forgotten all about the review. I scrunch my eyes closed, trying to focus back on what I'm supposed to be doing. But, no.

'Brochure, yes, we need both written and video brochures. Plus a corporate video brochure for corporate events – that should be hosted by Thalia. And speaking of Thalia, I recommend she is promoted to assistant staff manager to take a large workload off Diane. I think that's all for now. Oh yes, my review. I'm focusing on the Winter Wonderland activities.'

I start on my ice cream and look up to Shana. She's finished typing and is staring at me open-mouthed – whether due to my gibberish or sugar-fest, I don't know, and I'm too tired to worry. She busies herself completing her notes, so I finish my morning dessert and put my spoon down.

'Right, if there are no questions, could you update Diane when she returns please? I'm going to go and brainstorm some more, and I'll meet with her later to discuss. Thanks for your time; you've worked well. Good meeting.'

I go to my bedroom and sleep solidly for three hours.

***

I lie with my eyes closed, still in a cosy half-dreaming slumber. Then my heart races and my cheeks flush as I remember how my body quivered when his fingers trailed over my skin, and the shivers he sent down my back as he kissed my neck. The passion and emotion he conveyed in every kiss, and the profound wholeness I felt wrapped in his arms. Those tender cuddles touched my soul and set my spirit free. A wave of exhilaration surges through me and I squeal into my pillow, kicking my feet on the bed.

In my dreamy state, I reach for the complimentary resort-headed notepad and pen from the bedside table. I feel inspired to capture a snapshot of my heart after our night together.

I scrawl the feelings of this incredible high as quickly as they pop into my mind, not worrying about how they sound or if they make sense. These words are just for me, a record of this moment. When the flow of thoughts is all on the paper, I put down the pen and drift back into a blissful sleep.

Some time later, a falling sensation jolts me awake. My hand drops off the side of the bed, reaches into the pocket of the coat I left strewn on the floor, and pulls out my phone. I'm glad it is still working after its snow collision. I check the time. 'Diane!' I yell. I am so late. I've done nothing today. I throw on some clean clothes, splash some water on my face, and run out of the room.

I take the elevator down to the lobby, and as it nears the ground level, I see Lexi through the glass. When the doors open, she is walking towards me with tears streaming down her bright red face, being comforted by Nanny P. My heart doesn't know whether to beat faster or stop altogether.

'Darling, what's wrong?'

Lexi runs the final few steps and falls into my arms. I look up to Nanny P, who shrugs apologetically. I crouch down to her height. 'What's wrong, Lex?'

'I miss my dad,' she manages to say through her shuddering sobs.

'Oh, my darling.' I give her a tight squeeze. 'Let's go for a chat. I know just the place.'

I nod to Nanny P and silently mouth *thank you*. Lexi and I wrap our arms around each other and walk through the hotel lobby to the library snug.

'Grab some of those cushions, Lex, and we'll make a nest down here.' I bundle up some more cushions and a furry throw, and we nestle down in the corner.

Lexi and I sit cuddled up until her tears dry and her breathing calms. I reach up for a tissue from the table and pass it to her. For a fleeting moment, I recall all the crazy highs and lows that have gone before in this little space.

'What happened, my darling?' I pull her back into a tight hug. 'Come talk to me.'

Lexi squeezes the edge of the throw. 'All the other kids were playing with their dads and my dad isn't here. And he won't be with us at Christmas.'

'Oh, baby, I'm so sorry.' I hold her as more tears fill her eyes. 'I wish things could be different.' My heart aches for her. I know how it feels when parents break up and all dreams of having a happy family, however unrealistic, break too.

She looks up at me with her little lips turning downwards but her eyes wide. 'It's not your fault, Mum. I know if Dad was here, he'd be on his phone all the time.'

Her pain punches me in the gut, but I'm relieved to hear she's placing the blame with him – where it belongs. Lexi burrows her face in the throw to hide a muffled whisper, 'Sometimes I hate my dad.' She glances up, pulling at a loose thread. 'He never spends time with me.' Lexi bites her bottom lip, conflicted emotions playing across her face. 'But then I feel bad because I'm supposed to love my dad. And I do, but... I just wish he was different.'

I take her hand before she unravels the whole blanket. 'I know, my darling. It's OK to have those thoughts and feelings. I wish your dad was different too, but we can't change who he is or what he does. Only he can do that.' I stroke her hair and pause, trying to find the right, unbiased words to say. 'You haven't done anything wrong. Your dad loves you very much; he's just not very good at showing it. I hope you know that I will always love you and put you first.' She manages a small smile, and we snuggle up quietly for a while. I bury my face in her hair, wishing I could inhale all her sadness and transfer it to myself.

I have to put Lexi's needs first and do whatever is best for her – I just wish I knew what *would* be for the best with such limited options. But that's my role as a parent. Something that my mother never did – she always put herself first, always choosing her latest *gentleman caller* ahead of me. Although, they never acted like gentlemen towards her, or me. I was always an inconvenience and in the way. I will never let Lexi go through that.

'Do you feel ready to go back and play?'

Lexi nods, and I feel the excitement swell in her body. 'We're doing rehearsals for our performance this evening.' She turns to face me, her eyes piercing mine, full of fragile hope. 'You will come tonight, won't you?'

My breath catches. How many times have I broken promises, failed to show up when she needed me most? Each disappointment my own mother inflicted replays in my mind.

Not this time. I will move heaven and earth not to let my little girl down again.

'Of course I will, I promise,' I vow, my voice steady despite the swarm of doubts and insecurities plaguing my thoughts. But I cling to this purpose like a lifeline – I will be there for my daughter when no one was there for me.

We smile and hug again, and then she's ready to re-join the other children. *Please, gods of not letting your children down again, please don't let anything get in the way of tonight's performance.*

This must be the millionth time we've changed into our outdoor gear this week, and we race to do it at super speed. Lexi and I head outside towards the ballroom.

'What's the performance you're doing tonight?'

Lexi giggles, 'It's a surprise! We can't tell.'

'That makes it even more exciting. I can't wait.' We walk with our arms around each other, trying not to slip on the icy patches formed since the path was cleared this morning. When we arrive at the door, Lexi is raring to get inside and continue with rehearsals.

I hover in the doorway to make sure she settles. I glance around the hall, and my gaze settles on Jisung in his cream-coloured Prince Charming costume. My heart flutters, and I expect I have a daft, love-struck grin plastered on my face. I watch him teaching a small group of young boys some dance steps. The boys look focused and determined, and when they look up, their teacher ruffles their hair, proud of their achievements. My smile drifts away at what should be, and is, a heart-warming sight. But my shoulders drop and a small voice inside my head reminds me that Jisung is several years younger than me and wants a family of his own. Could there really be a future for us?

I turn away and walk outside, needing fresh air. The real world has crept inside the resort and slapped me round the face a few times today. Fairy-Tale Wonderland should be all rainbows and flowers, not shit dads and out-of-date ovaries. I wish I hadn't got out of bed. I should have stayed cosied up in my dream world.

And I still have to face Diane, knowing I've done no work apart from garble some ideas that she didn't even ask for. And I have been asleep most of the day. I'm in deep trouble, but I better go and face the showdown.

***

The door is closed when I arrive at Diane's office. I tap lightly, inwardly praying to the procrastination gods that she still isn't there. I hear no reply, and then the door opens. Diane looks... fragile. Her shoulders are humped and she looks small without her heels on – she's not even wearing any make-up. She gestures for me to come in and sit while she continues to pace the length of her office. I'm gripped by a sudden fear that I'm about to be sent home.

'Is everything all right, Diane?' I ask quietly, not wanting to interrupt. She stops and looks at me as if she's only just noticed I'm in the room.

'Cally, sorry, where are my manners?' She opens the door and calls out, 'Coffee, please.'

She picks up a brochure from her desk and hands it to me. Holding my breath, waiting for the bad news, I glance down. *Sun Valley Nursing Home.* I wait for her to make comparisons or shout, or... something.

'Frank and I went to visit this morning.' She sits next to me on the couch. 'How does it look to you?'

I don't understand what she's asking of me. 'The brochure?'

'The home. We are considering Frank moving to Sun Valley.'

Her eyes fill with tears, and without time to process what she said, I shuffle closer and put my arm around her shoulder. She rests her head against me, and her shoulders begin to shudder. I pull her into a hug just as Shana opens the door to bring in the tray of coffee. I mouth, 'Thank you,' and Shana nods and disappears back out of the room.

Diane stands to collect some tissues and I pour the coffee. We both heave a sigh.

'I don't know what to do,' Diane says, drying her eyes. 'He's been my rock for so many years, but I can't cope with managing the resort and looking after him. He needs more and more care. I want to be there for him, but...'

'Oh, Diane, I'm so sorry. I didn't realise things had got this bad for you. I wish there was some way I could help.'

She pats my shoulder. 'It helps with you being here.' She manages a small smile and sits back down with her cup. 'It's hard making it on your own, as you know.'

I take hold of her hand. 'It is, but you have a great team behind you here, and I'm sure Frank would be very well looked after. You could visit often and enjoy his company.'

She looks me in the eyes, and her voice lowers to a whisper. 'How do I let go of someone I love?'

Her comment resonates far more than she would ever know. We sit quietly for a while, both thinking over that same question, but our situations are at opposite ends of a relationship timeline.

Diane drains her coffee. 'I hear good things from Shana about your meeting this morning. I'm sorry I haven't had time to go over the notes. We'll meet tomorrow, if that's all right with you?'

We end our brief sort-of meeting with a hug. It almost makes me laugh that she, the resort manager, is apologising and seeking agreement from me, a lowly visitor. Then again, she hasn't read the notes yet. I barely even remember the drivel I came out with this morning.

I leave Diane's office in a state of unease; it's been an unsettling week, and I need to clear my head. I casually pick up a cushion from a throne as I walk out of the hotel and head to the Secret Garden. It has become my place of solitude and contemplation in a hectic resort full of people, timetables, activity, and bustle. I need a holiday to recover from this holiday. And quite frankly, I need a break from adulting and to reconnect with the magic of this place.

I wander through to the little island at the garden's centre and to the little bench, upon which I place my borrowed cushion. There, now I can sit and think without getting a cold bottom and hemorrhoids. I sit down and roll back my shoulders, quite proud of my foresight and ingenuity. This movement reveals the pain of tight muscles in my neck and shoulders where stress has taken hold. I roll my head to loosen up and catch a glimpse of the rose in the glass dome. I forgot to look up its meaning after I saw it at the beginning of the week. Now the stem is bare, its red petals shrivelling at the base. It's strange that the gardeners haven't replaced it.

Maybe the rose isn't connected to a fairy tale, but a lesson about nature. Nature grows and flourishes and then withers and dies before it rests and renews. Like the cycle of the seasons. Like my marriage. And now I'm in the rest and renewal stage. Ugh! It doesn't feel very restful. Or very warm – even with a cushion. I begin the walk back to the hotel, shaking out my arms and legs before I get frostbite.

Maybe that's what life is all about – not fingers and toes falling off, but growing and changing, letting things take their natural course. I spy the little robin who I swear is following me along the path. 'What do you think, robin? Perhaps I don't need to know all the answers beforehand, do I?' He flutters to another branch and tweets his tuneful call. *'The future is promised to no one.* That's very true. I have to make the most of the time I have here.' Another robin joins our conversation with its twitter. 'You robins are surprisingly insightful. *See where my journey leads.* Hmm, well, my journey here led me to fall into a love I didn't know I wanted.' I stop still. Wait, I don't mean *love* love. Do I?

THURSDAY

Solo

As I sit in the back row of the audience, my insides are churning and even my hands are trembling. I fidget with the sweet program the children have created and strain in the darkness to see Lexi's name written inside.

'Are you all right, dear?' Diane whispers, placing a kind hand on my knee.

'I'm so nervous for her. Honestly, anyone would think I was the one having to go up on stage and sing by myself.'

'She'll shine like a star. You'll see.'

I turn my head with a slow smile. 'Thank you for coming with me this evening.'

'My pleasure.' Diane takes hold of my hand. 'You're right; I did need to take some time out.'

I turn my hand to give hers a comforting squeeze. 'You deserve a break.' It's lovely to see her looking more relaxed and back to her glamorous self.

A young man in a tuxedo walks along our row to hand Diane and I a glass of champagne each. 'Gosh, we don't get comfy chairs and waiters with champagne in the school hall – such a treat!' I chuckle.

'All the children get a special supper backstage too, and we have the nannies and fairies to help the little ones with any pre-show anxiety.' She smiles proudly – she must be behind all the special touches for the evening. I spot a team of photographers setting up their equipment at the front. 'I do appreciate not having all the parents with their phones in the air trying to take photos of their kids; it will make a change to be able to see.'

'Yes, I can imagine.' Diane looks down for a moment and smooths down her uncrinkled dress. 'The photographers have been taking photos all day so the little ones will get their own special memento to take home.' She smiles but doesn't look in my direction as she speaks.

And then it dawns on me – times like this must be especially hard for her after losing her daughter. I cough back the lump in my throat and take a sip of my drink. I'm such an idiot for asking her to come. What was I thinking? I can't begin to relate to the pain she must be feeling. I put my arm around her shoulder, and she nods a little. She probably doesn't want me to notice her taking a tissue from her bag and dabbing her eyes. I give her shoulder a squeeze. I wish I had some words that might bring some comfort.

Excited giggles sound from behind the stage curtains and a little girl's face peeps between, making the audience laugh. The music begins, and the curtains slowly open. The stage is set as a sparkling winter woodland, complete with trees and fake snow on the ground. A boy of about Lexi's age is standing in the centre, smartly dressed in a white shirt with a red bow tie.

'Ladies and gentlemen, may I present… A Fairy-Tale Christmas.' He sweeps out his arm to the stage and walks to the side. He pauses, surveying the audience with his hand shielding his eyes from the bright stage lights. A woman in the audience stands and waves, and her hands usher him to continue. He waves back with a huge grin and then begins to narrate the story.

Onto the stage comes a line of the youngest children, dressed in white fairy costumes with glittering little wings. There's a hushed *awww* from the audience, which increases in volume as the tiny fairies perform their dance. They're all out of sync and have forgotten most of their steps, which makes them even more adorable. Tears spring to my eyes and I fight the urge to cry my eyes out. My hand flies to my overwhelmed heart. I don't even know these children and yet this is quite possibly the cutest thing I have ever seen. Diane hands me a tissue. 'I think we'll both need more than one of these.' She's laughing a little, with tears already streaming down her cheeks. She nods to one of the staff standing at the back of the hall, who then hands out boxes of tissues to each row of parents.

The performance continues with the children in marvellous costumes, making jokes, fluffing their lines, dancing, and singing their little hearts out. Parents laugh and clap along to their heart-warming tale of Christmas spirit, kindness, and hope. I watch in nervous anticipation of Lexi's solo, which doesn't come until the very end.

She walks confidently to the centre of the stage with a beaming smile, exquisitely dressed as an angel. She sings an acapella, hauntingly beautiful song with the sweetest melody and lyrics that summarise the lovely themes of the story. The audience is silent, hanging on to every word that she delivers perfectly. I am standing to get the best view, an emotional wreck, blubbering throughout and saturating numerous tissues. My proud mummy heart is overspilling with love and joy.

At the end, Lexi curtsies and the audience immediately raises in a standing ovation. She soaks up the roar of cheers and claps, and I can see in her smile that she's proud of herself. My chest hurts from my heart bursting, my hands throb from clapping so hard, my eyes are sore, and I have tears dripping from my chin and snot hanging from my nose. She would be so embarrassed if she could see me now.

When the clapping subsides and Lexi exits the spotlight, Jisung walks onto the stage, dressed in his Prince Charming finery. I'm not sure how much more my heart can expand before I die on the spot.

'Ladies and gentlemen, it has been a pleasure to work with your children this week. I am proud of them all for the effort they have made to put on this production in a short amount of time. Please join me in giving the children a big round of applause.'

I'm sure Lexi is beaming even brighter backstage hearing that Prince Charming is proud of her. While we watch the children all file on stage for their final bows, something tickles my neck. I look around, and Jisung is standing behind me with his finger to his lips.

I surreptitiously glance at Diane to check she didn't notice. Thankfully she is standing, clapping for the cast. Slow, sensual strokes of my hair and shoulders send shivers down my spine. My heart is racing, fearful of getting caught while also wanting to leap on him. Then he leans in to kiss my neck and whispers, 'How do you fancy a secret illicit rendezvous? Eight o'clock in the lobby?'

I look round, my eyes wide, stunned that he remembers my exact words from the summer ball – a scene I have played over in my mind a million times. His sultry expression makes me gasp and bite my lip. Then he wiggles his eyebrows at me and I struggle to hold in my laughter. I wink as my reply, and he casually strolls back to the stage for photographs with the kids.

My excitement is brought to an abrupt halt when I feel the vibration of my phone ringing inside my bag. Horrified at breaking the rules when sitting next to the resort owner, I make rapid apologies and dash out of the door.

A brief glance at the screen shows the caller is... my literary agent?

'Hello?'

'Cally? It's Christine Charlbury. I'm sorry to phone this late and while you're away, but I have urgent news. And I think you're going to like it.'

I walk down the corridor to a quieter space and turn my back to hide my rule-breaking. 'I'm intrigued. Go on.'

'I've received correspondence from Brahms and Langford. They're a smaller independent publisher... they want to offer you a publishing deal.'

I stop dead. 'You're joking me.'

'Not at all. They love your Cinderella retelling and the concept for the rest of the series. They want to publish all six titles.'

I fall back against the wall, feeling the blood drain from my face. 'Oh my...'

'I'll negotiate the best deal for you once they reopen after the Christmas break, but they've already offered a decent five-figure sum, with a thirty percent advance as soon as you sign. Congratulations, Cally Jackson, soon-to-be published author!'

I'm frozen to the spot. I feel numb, but my hands are shaking. 'I don't know what to say. I think I'm in shock. *Thank you* doesn't seem enough.'

'Enjoy your Christmas break. You've got a busy year ahead.'

'Merry Christmas, Christine. Thank you again.'

I hang up and stare into space. My heart is pounding as if I've been running for forty-two years and finally reached my destination. I've only gone and bloody done it! A warmth in my chest that I don't recognise spreads up to my lips and forms a grin so wide, it hurts my cheeks. I think, for the first time in my life, I feel proud of myself. I have accomplished something unimaginable by myself, for myself. And… most important of all, I may well have saved Lexi and I from our housing crisis. Dreams really can come true!

***

Nanny P accompanies Lexi and I in the elevator as we head back to our room. Lexi has passed through her excited babbling phase and is now tired and over-emotional. I hold her in a hug. 'Are you sure you're OK to put our little superstar to bed?'

Nanny P nods, her eyes still red. 'It would be my pleasure. We've had a wonderful day, haven't we, Lexi?'

Lexi turns and hugs Nanny P. 'I couldn't have done it without you.'

I hold back a giggle at her theatrical tone, which sounds like an awards acceptance speech. A diva in the making, I fear and admire. 'I think someone needs an early night.'

Lexi immediately perks up. 'But I'm not tired! We can read lots of stories, can't we, Nanny P?'

'It's Christmas Eve tomorrow. We've got another busy day ahead and the ball in the evening.' This was the wrong thing for me to say – it seems to have given Lexi an extra boost of bubbly energy, and she dances her way to our room.

I leave the two of them to read together while I take a quick shower. Two dates in one week – I could get used to this! I race to get ready, my stomach full of excited butterflies and only a few fluttering with nerves. Although I face the same old nothing-to-wear issue, I manage to find underwear that isn't fraying and even matches!

Ohmygosh! Perhaps I could spend a tiny amount of my advance on some new clothes? I let out a sudden gasp of horror at my reflection in the mirror, hands hovering over my head as I dry my hair… I might have to do public appearances, like book signings, and have my own photoshoot.

'What's up, Mum?'

'Nothing, I was just thinking about work.' I'm holding off telling Lexi my news – tonight is her night in the spotlight. She jumps up and skips over to me, providing a welcome interruption to my impending anxiety attack.

'Can I do your make-up?'

'Err…'

'I'll do it nicely, I promise.'

She looks at me with her puppy-dog eyes and flutters her eyelashes. She knows I can't resist when she looks so cute.

'Go on, then.'

Admittedly, when she's finished, I don't look like I've stepped out of the 80s. But I draw the line at her applying my mascara so I don't end up looking like a goth… or needing an eye hospital. As I put in my sparkly earrings, Lexi puts her arms around me. 'You look beautiful, Mum.'

'Awww, thank you, my darling.' I give her a big goodnight kiss. She's still my sweet little girl beneath her tweenage sass. And with that little confidence boost, I'm ready to leave.

In the elevator, I rub at my cheeks – I blush more than enough when I'm with Jisung, so I don't need any additional pink. Especially not the amount Lexi applied. I wonder what Jisung's idea of an illicit rendezvous is. Hopefully it doesn't include any ice baths. I put on my outdoor gear and wait by the hotel entrance.

I don't have to wait long before there is a pat on my bottom as Jisung walks past and out of the door. I swing around to check no one in the lobby noticed, breathe a sigh of relief, and follow him outside.

At the bottom of the staircase, he grabs my hand and runs through the snow, pulling me behind him. I let out a squeal of surprise and fear. It's snowing hard and I have no doubt that if I fell, I would have ten broken bones for Christmas. 'Stop!' I yell, breathless from the unexpected exertion. He comes to a stop once we're on a more secluded path surrounded by trees. He lifts me off the ground and spins around, making me squeal again. Laughing, he lets me slowly slide down, kissing me on the nose on my way back to the ground. I keep my arms wrapped around him, and he cups my face to kiss me.

'Mmmm, I've missed your lips.' He narrows his eyes and kisses me several more times.

I'm already weak at the knees. 'Where are you taking me?'

He raises an eyebrow in the most seductive manner, and I laugh at how he has construed my words.

'You'll see.'

Uh oh, I've heard those words before. Ice bath in the snow, here we come.

We continue trudging down the path, snowflakes melting into our hair.

'Is it far? We're getting wet.'

He stops and looks at me with mischief in his eyes. 'Wet, you say?'

Before I can react, his arms are around my body and he jumps backwards into the deep snow. I scream as I fall on top of him. He provides a soft landing and holds me tight as he rolls us in the snow, both of us laughing like naughty children.

'Yes, wet!' I grab the first handful of snow. Neither of us holds back in our snowball fight, trying to splatter each other's faces until my stomach hurts from laughing and we're both soaked. We collapse in a cuddle and lie wrapped in each other's arms on the cold, snowy ground, catching snowflakes on our tongues.

'You have strange ideas for dates.' I laugh. 'I haven't played in the snow for years. I forgot how fun it is.'

He leans over me and kisses the snowflakes on my eyelids. 'We haven't got to our date yet.' He jumps up and pulls me to my feet. 'Let's go and warm up. I don't want you to catch a cold.'

I shiver. 'Sounds good to me.'

A little further ahead, we come to a wooden cabin. There are no lights on, no one around. I stare at the big sign over the door: *Santa's Grotto*. 'Seriously? We can't go in there! It feels like... I don't know, unholy.'

'I cleared it with Santa; he gave me the key.' With a chuckle, Jisung produces an oversized golden key from his pocket and unlocks the door. He goes inside and switches on the fire, which emits a soft, golden glow that illuminates the room. I follow him in and lock the door behind me. We leave our boots on the mat and start stripping off our soaked jackets and trousers, hanging them on the backs of chairs to dry.

Standing on the soft rug in just my underwear and jumper, I rub my legs, trying to warm up by the fire.

'One day, we should have a date where we keep our clothes on.'

'Where's the fun in that?' He laughs and opens a bottle of champagne.

'Did Santa leave that for us?'

He nods towards the table. 'Look, he left us a gift too.'

He tosses the gift box to me and I juggle it awkwardly before carefully unpeeling the tape. 'Ex-tra la-rge,' I slowly sound out as the text is partially revealed. Curiosity piqued, I tear the paper and a box falls into my lap. 'Condoms!'

I gasp my loudest ever gasp. My hands fly up to cover my face, which I can feel has turned as red as Santa's hat hanging by the fireplace. Jisung howls with belly-clutching laughter, watching me die of embarrassment. It takes a good while before I can peel my hands from my flushed cheeks. He passes my glass and I hold it against each cheek to cool the burning mortification

Shaking my head, I sit next to a still-chuckling Jisung on the couch by the window. The cabin warms up quickly, and for a while we're both hypnotised by the flickering flames that dance in the hearth. Around the walls are framed photos of Santa's reindeer, and with the fresh pine scent of the real Christmas tree and its twinkling coloured lights, the atmosphere is magical.

When I can eventually face the man sitting next to me, it feels like a dream. Even more so when I glance down to his bare, muscular thighs. In fact, it suddenly feels quite warm, and I have to take off my jumper. I swivel my legs up onto the couch and sit on my knees.

'Something amazing happened, and I wanted to tell you first.'

He raises his eyebrows, inviting me to tell my news.

'I don't know if you remember from the summer, I told you I wanted to write children's books…' I pause and take a sip of my drink.

'Of course, that was your dream. I said you should go for it.'

Oh my heart, he remembers. 'Well… I did it. And I can't believe I'm going to say this, but I got a phone call this evening…'

He leans forward, a smile waiting on his lips.

'I got a publishing deal. I'm going to be a real published author.' A huge grin bursts onto my face as I say the words out loud. Jisung throws his arms around me and pulls me onto his lap, giving me the biggest hug I've ever received.

'Congratulations, Cally. I am so proud of you.'

I stroke his smooth cheek. 'I wouldn't have tried if you hadn't encouraged me.'

'Sure you would. Maybe at a different time, but you would have got there.'

'You have more confidence in me than I do.'

'We must celebrate!' He lifts me back onto the couch and stands up to refill our glasses. 'To your future success.'

I stand up to chink his glass. 'Thank you, and to yours.'

With one arm holding me against him, he kisses my forehead. 'Ah no, tonight is all for you.'

'It means I can get somewhere for me and Lexi to live.'

He puts down both of our glasses and hugs me tight. 'I knew you were a badass.' He kisses me on the lips and runs his fingers down my spine – smiling as it makes me shiver. Skin against skin, our bodies are practically sizzling.

I reach for my drink to cool my rising temperature. When I turn back, Jisung is sitting on Santa's big, comfy armchair.

'You can't sit there! That's Santa's chair!'

'Don't be shy.' He pats his thigh. 'Come and sit on my lap.'

'No, that's so wrong!'

'I want to give you a Christmas treat.'

'We can't!'

'Why, have you been a naughty girl?'

He smirks and runs his thumb along his lower lip, which has me clutching at my imaginary pearls, and I'm not proud of the lustful facial expression I make in return. He reaches out his hand and winks. 'You wanted illicit…'

***

Sometime later… I kneel on the couch and peer through the curtains, wiping the condensation to see outside. It's stopped snowing, and the skies are beginning to clear. Relaxing back on the couch next to me, Jisung skims his palm down the back of my leg. 'Do we have time for more treats?' His voice is low and husky, and I can't wait to hear him speak to me like that again.

I stroke the hair from his eyes. 'Sadly not. I need to start heading back to Lexi for midnight.' I can feel my lips pouting. 'Tonight's not long enough.' I turn around and snuggle into Jisung's arms. 'This is where I want to be.'

He strokes my back. 'This week's not long enough.'

I press my body against his, gripping him to me. I don't want to let go – now, or ever. The pain of having to leave him in the summer lingers in the back of my mind, coming closer to the forefront as the week progresses.

I nestle into his neck, fighting the urge to bite his smooth skin. I can feel he's up for more treats, and it's already getting too hard to resist. 'Will I see you tomorrow?'

'I have meetings all day, but I'll get away as soon as I can. What are your plans?'

'I have a mountain of work and want to have some fun with Lexi.' My body stiffens and Jisung holds me tighter. The words go unspoken, but I'm sure he's thinking it too. Our commitments and responsibilities make it difficult enough to carve out time for each other, even when we're in the same place.

I look up into his eyes, knowing this is an issue we need to talk about, but without any answers, I don't think either of us wants to speak about the future. I kiss him instead, putting off the inevitable conversation to prolong the enjoyment of the present moment.

We dress back into our warm but damp outdoor clothes and lock up the cabin as we leave. Arm in arm, we kick through the fresh snow and admire the stars that are now bright in the sky.

'That one there.' He points above the tip of the palace. 'The North star, the brightest star in the sky.' He reaches around my shoulders and pulls me to him. 'At times, the star may be hidden from sight, but it's always there. That's where we'll find each other when we're apart.'

My insides jolt. 'Now we've found each other, I don't want to think about us being apart again.'

'I know.' He squeezes my shoulder and kisses the top of my head.

I snuggle up close. 'I know it sounds stupid, but do you believe in destiny?' I peek up to see his reaction.

He meets my gaze and nods. 'I do, yeah. It's hard not to after finding you here.' We look into each other's eyes with smiles that say a million words. Which still wouldn't be enough to convey what's in my heart.

We stop walking before we lose our privacy in the open space of the village green. His hand cradles the back of my neck and he pulls me into a cuddle. 'I really am proud of you, you know. You had a dream and you made it real. That shows strength and courage. You inspire me.'

He sounds sincere, and I have to look away, blinking fast. 'Don't, you'll make me cry. I'm not used to anyone saying such nice things to me.' That's difficult to realise and sad to admit.

He gently holds my cheek and turns my head to face him again. 'I'm going to change that.' He kisses my forehead, making me sigh as I open myself to the peace and security that he gives.

'You didn't even need a Prince Charming to save you!' There's humour in his voice, but I sense an undercurrent to his words – maybe a relief that I don't want him for his money? That I want him for the man he is underneath all the material fluff that isn't important to me?

'You think maybe...' My mouth is dry and I swallow hard. 'I don't know how to explain without sounding soft.'

'Life has made you tough, Cally, but it's OK to be soft. You can share what's in your heart. Your feelings are safe with me.'

I nod. He's right. It does feel safe to be soft with him, and I want to open my heart. 'You think maybe we met to see each other for who we are inside? Like two souls that were searching for each other. Maybe we're here to save each other.'

FRIDAY

Christmas Magic

Cosy socks on, I put my feet up on the couch and rest back on the plump cushions. Lexi's enthusiasm to rise early so she doesn't miss a second of today's kids' club activities meant I snagged the most coveted couch in the guest lounge.

I'm in a writer's winter paradise. My own private corner hideaway, the morning sun streaming through its large, round window overlooking the snowy landscape. And with staff on hand to provide unlimited coffee. And snacks.

All I need now is a brainwave. I know what I need to do: write a review that glows so bright, it will be seen by all the affluent family holidaymakers in the world. On a practical level, I have no idea how to do that.

That's not quite true. I do know the largest publication for our target market. And it's going to take some seriously brave badassery to contact them. I daren't even *think* its name, let alone say it out loud, in case it puts a curse on me or something sinister.

How do I make my review the glowiest? I'm not even sure 'glowiest' is a real word. Not a good start.

Cup of coffee in hand, I poise my pen over the blank page, determined to make meaningful progress on this review.

To Do:
Write Winter Wonderland Review.

Starting strong, not only do I have words on paper, but I'm on my second page already. My self-satisfied sip of coffee tastes like victory.

FIRST DRAFT
Winter Wonderland at
Fairy-Tale Wonderland –
A Review
by Cally Jackson

Step into the magical... Hmm, maybe enchantment sounds better? Step into the enchantment... No, wait! Experience the enchantment... Maybe mind-boggling? Or perhaps magical?

Hmm, maybe it should be something like: Make magical memories or unforgettable memories that will blow your socks off! Or... memories of utterly incredible or jaw-dropping wonder in an enchanting Fairy-Tale Winter Wonderland.

Oh, who am I kidding? This is harder than quantum physics! Ugh! I need cake. Me brain no worky. I have the right words; I just need to put them in the right order. I add 'drink coffee and eat breakfast' to my to-do list. And then cross those off.

I'm well underway now and have already completed two thirds of the tasks on my to-do list, so I'm feeling accomplished. It must be time for a break. I stand up and stretch, gazing out over the grounds. It really is the most beautiful view – enchanting, exciting, stunning, peaceful, picturesque... All words I need to quickly jot down.

Hmm... Maybe it's not my review that needs to be glowy. The resort is already the glowiest. The winter wonderland speaks for itself. It's not like I need to make anything up. I just need to capture what's here in words. Oh, brain, thank you. That sounds much easier. Let's celebrate with coffee.

> *Fairy-Tale Wonderland is the perfect place to reconnect with your loved ones and create your very own fairy-tale winter wonderland.*

That's the final sentence complete!

I just need to write the beginning and middle now. Which is impossible because we haven't experienced all of the week's activities yet and the week keeps getting better and better. Lexi's with the elves this morning, and we've still got the Winter Ball to come, and meeting Santa. And I'm sure Christmas Day will be spectacular.

> *From the moment I stepped through the magical entrance... Blah blah blah.*

> *Then we did some cool Christmassy stuff.*

Ugh. The deadline is looming, people are depending on me, there are a whole heap of serious consequences if I fail, and I must avenge the damage caused by my nemesis, Miss Suit. But I still can't get this finished today.

It must surely be almost lunchtime. I've been at this for hours. I call over a member of staff carrying a jug of coffee. As she pours my cup of delicious, energising elixir, I ask the time.

'It's nine-thirty, madam.'

I slump back onto the couch, thoroughly disheartened and wanting to wail with self-pity. But giving up is not an option.

I soon find my feet on the couch, and I've settled in a comfortable horizontal position. It's not long before I'm staring out of the window, daydreaming of last night, and my treats...

And to think, if I'd stayed with Ben, I would never have known how thrilling and fun 'it' can be when I'm not under duress. Or how fun life can be. With tingles inside and a smile on my face, my eyes accidentally close.

'Excuse me, madam. Would you like a fresh cup of coffee?'

'Wah!' Eyes wide, I sit bolt upright, sending my notebook and pen flying. It takes a second to compose myself. 'Sorry, just resting my eyes. That would be lovely, thank you. Do you have the time, please?' The corner of my mouth feels tight as I speak. I rub away the dried drool while my coffee is poured.

'Time for elevenses, madam.'

Another morning wasted.

***

With excitement rising in my chest, I follow the *Santa's Workshop* signs to the kids' club hall, eager to experience the magic with Lexi. When I go through the door, it's as if I have been whisked away to the North Pole and am now standing inside Santa's actual workshop. The events team has outdone themselves, transforming the hall with oversized baubles and nutcrackers and brightly wrapped gift boxes to create an enchanting setting for the morning's activities.

The children, each wearing elf hats and aprons, are seated along rows of benches, their little hands busy assembling their very own Santa Express train kits and stuffing their fluffy teddy bears. As they work, they erupt into giggles at the silly antics of the elf staff, who sing and dance along to the festive music playing in the background.

Lexi is intently focused on making her bear and doesn't notice me coming in. She looks extra cute with rosy cheeks and freckles painted around her red nose. When I manage to catch her eye, I give her a wave, and she makes her bear's paw wave back, looking so proud of her creation.

I join the other parents, who are gathered around the sides of the room, beaming with pride as they watch the excitement on their children's faces. The air is filled with Christmas cheer and the whole scene is a joy to witness, making me feel all warm and fuzzy.

This is what Fairy-Tale Wonderland does best: making the magic come alive for both kids and parents.

Now *that* is an awesome sentence to include, maybe highlight, in my review. I scramble to take the notepad out of my bag and quickly write down the words before I forget them. Chest a little puffed, I read it back to myself. Although… it sounds somewhat familiar.

Oh, sparkly frickin' elf dust. I think I've read it before in the resort brochure.

That's it. I am switching off my mental computer and checking out of work for the rest of the day.

The children's energy is at an all-time high as the elves' toy-making session draws to a close. They sing along with a lively and hilarious song, and even the parents can't resist joining in with silly actions. By the end, everyone is in fits of laughter. The children thank the staff with special nose twitches and secret elf handshakes, and we all leave in high festive spirits.

***

Squeals of delight sound from the dining hall as the children enter into a magical candy cane forest. Huge candy canes are planted like trees around the hall, creating a stripy maze that we wander through to get to our dining tables. The air is thick with the sweet scent of peppermint, and the look of wonder on Lexi's face as she explores her way around is priceless.

As we settle at our table, adorned in festive red and white with glittering baubles and candy cane place settings, the sound of laughing and chatting fills the room. The candy-cane-inspired menu goes down a treat while the children share stories and giggle about the morning's elf mischief, building their anticipation of the afternoon ahead.

Once our tables have been cleared, the elves reappear, taking us all by surprise and causing utter mayhem. They bounce in like hyperactive kangaroos, whooping and cheering, one juggling flaming candy canes, others showering us with confetti. Balloons fly across the room along with handfuls of candies, whipping the children into a frenzy of excitement. They clown around each table, greeting us with their nose twitching and secret handshakes.

One of the elves stands up front and does a funny jig that has the children in stitches, then somehow manages to get them to hush for an announcement.

'It's time for a cookie decorating competition! We've got lots of prizes for you to win.' The children all cheer. 'You have twenty minutes to decorate the…'

Another elf shouts through a megaphone, 'Best cookie ever!'

A third elf leaps around, bells jingling, yelling, 'Don't let us put you off!'

Lexi turns to me, looking anxious. 'They won't tickle us, will they?'

'No, I'm sure they won't.' They better not anyway. I can't be held responsible for where my fists and elbows fly if I'm tickled.

One of the mums at our table starts to rummage through the basket we've been given, taking out cookies and decorations, but only for herself and her child. Me and the other mums then dive at the basket like it's a mega Black Friday sale, on a mission to gather our own supplies. When we all sit ready to begin, there are narrow-eyed stares.

Well, if it's a cookie war they want, I shall roll up my sleeves and narrow my eyes too. All in the spirit of good will, of course.

We lay out our cookies and sprinkles in front of us, and Lexi bounces in her seat. 'This will be so much fun.'

I grab an elf hat and yank it down over my hair. 'Let's win those prizes, Lex.'

She gives me a *don't be embarrassing* side glance, which I ignore, and I stretch back my fingers in preparation. Lexi sings, 'I'm going to make–'

'Shhh! Keep your plans top secret!'

The megaphone makes a deafening screech, and the elf giggles. 'Are you ready to become the ultimate cookie champion? Ready, set, decorate!'

The room springs into decorating action. Our table is almost silent.

'Mum, please can you pass the mini marshmallows? I'm going to make a snowman.' Lexi's voice is barely audible. Good girl.

I smother my cookie with frosting and, using a toothpick, begin my snowflake pattern. I'm not finding it as easy as it looked in the video clip I once saw. Smoothing over the frosting, I start again.

The elves run amok around the tables, pulling faces, telling jokes, and blowing horns. There are giggles around the room, but our table remains focused.

As the minutes tick by, I'm getting increasingly frustrated with smoothing and starting over. Lexi's happily alternating putting a marshmallow on her cookie with putting one in her mouth.

'Five more minutes!' yells Megaphone Elf, walking on his hands.

Just as I start to think I should change my design idea, Lexi yelps, tears about to spill. I immediately worry she may be about to vomit with excitement. 'Are you all right?'

'I've run out of marshmallows.' Her bottom lip quivers as she searches through the basket. 'There aren't any left.'

I stare aghast at her beautiful snowman with a glaring gap in his snow belly. Before I have time to panic and before a single teardrop falls, the young boy beside Lexi holds out his hand with marshmallows in his palm. 'Here, you can have mine.'

While his mum yells, 'Wait!' Lexi gives the boy a big hug, and he helps her fill in the missing pieces. Her face lights up with gratitude, and my heart melts. As they praise each other's creations, the other parents also stop to watch.

I look around the table at a few uncomfortable expressions and awkward shuffles, and smile. 'We can learn a lot from our kids.'

'Thirty seconds left!'

With renewed perspective, everyone makes their finishing touches. Apart from me, who has to start from scratch. I throw on all the coloured sprinkles we have to make a festive, err, glitter ball.

'Time's up!' calls Megaphone Elf. 'Pants down! Whoops! I mean, cookies down!'

The children all laugh and scoff the leftover decorations as the elves circle round, judging each cookie. They make a big show of deliberating, making exaggerated expressions of approval for kids or disgust for parents.

'And the winner is… drumroll, please…' Megaphone Elf pauses for dramatic effect while everyone stamps their feet.

Funny Jig Elf interrupts. 'Every kid's a winner!'

The children all cheer as the elves give out prizes. Only one mum at our table grumbles, prompting a stern glare from her daughter.

Funny Jig Elf approaches our table and does a funny jig, of course. Then he hands a gold envelope each to Lexi and the boy beside her. 'These are special prizes for showing kindness and friendship. Congratulations, little elves.' He pretends to knock their heads together, then whispers in their ears as we all clap. The two of them beam proudly.

With the widest smile, and her eyes full of awe, Lexi comes to sit on my lap.

'Well done, my darling.' I squeeze her tight. 'What did he say to you?'

She turns, her gaze twinkling with magic, and gently brushes my hair aside, whispering behind her hand, 'He said we were at the top of Santa's nice list.' My heart swells. 'But it's a secret.' She places her finger over her lips, and I stifle a chuckle. 'Can I put this in your bag please, Mum? I'll open it later so the other kids won't feel left out.' My heart swells even more.

***

Back in Santa's Workshop, a curtain is pulled back to reveal our afternoon's special visitor. The darkened stage is set as a quaint cottage living room with a roaring fire. A soft spotlight falls over Mrs Claus, sitting in a rocking chair in front of the fireplace. She looks exactly as we imagine with gold, round-rimmed spectacles at the end of her nose, wearing a frilly white bonnet and pinny, and with the kindliest face.

The children are awestruck and huddle around, sitting cross-legged on the floor as close to her as possible. They each have a cup of hot chocolate and munch on their cookies, mesmerised as she tells a story about the elves and their gingerbread house.

Parents sit around the back with welcome cups of coffee and mince pies. From the number of closed eyes and temples being rubbed, I think we all feel relieved to have a little peace and quiet after the chaos caused by those naughty elves. Quite honestly, I'm shocked the children are sitting so quietly after their sugar rush.

When the story ends and Mrs Claus has answered the children's questions, the noisy elves arrive with wide brooms to sweep us all outside. Mrs Claus waves us goodbye, and as we pass closer on our way out, there's something about her smile that reminds me of Diane. But my feet are brushed towards the door before I can properly see if it really is her beneath the floppy cap.

We head out into the snow in fits of laughter, dazzled by the bright sunlight. The children are like coiled springs being released, full of energy they've been politely holding in.

As the kids rush off to play tag, my eyes are suddenly covered by the cold fingers of someone from behind. My heart skips, and before I can turn, I'm lifted off the ground and whizzed around the corner out of view.

I stop giggling when Jisung pins me against the wall, pressing his lips urgently against mine and kissing me with a fervour that sends my heart racing. His breath is hot and fast in my ear as he pulls my collar aside to trail his mouth to my neck, sucking the sweet spot that makes me groan with desire.

My fingers tangle in his soft hair, pulling the back of his head closer as he gently bites. Right now, I don't care if he marks my skin or even if we're caught. Just hearing him moan into my neck sends me to another level of lust I've never experienced before. I can't think straight as Jisung's lips leave a trail of heat on my skin. All I know is I want more.

Leaving me breathing furiously, Jisung kisses my cheek and smirks. 'Sorry we're not against a tree. I hope the wall will do.'

'I'm surprised the snow hasn't melted.' I straighten my coat and shake back my hair. 'But I think we should try it again some time, just to check it meets my fantasy requirements.'

'Any time.' Jisung laughs and puts his arm around me. 'Shall we go and play with Lexi?'

'Really? Do you have time?'

'My meetings finished early.' He pulls his fleece neck warmer up over his mouth and takes a woolly hat from his pocket. With a muffled laugh, he says, 'I'll have to wear a disguise. Prince Charming can't be seen to have favourites. Ready to go?'

I nod, thrilled we can play in public. I just hope Lexi doesn't say anything to get us caught.

***

'Mum, Mum, Mum! We have to build a snowman to win a prize. The competition is about to start.' Lexi takes my hand, pulling me towards the crowd. She glances up at the man beside me, her eyes growing wider as she tries to recognise the nose between his woollen layers. She pulls my arm to whisper, 'Who's that?'

I haven't thought this through. Do I tell her Jisung isn't really a prince?

'Pssst! Lexi!' Jisung whispers, crouching down. 'It's me, Prince Charming.' He covertly uncovers his face for a second and puts his finger to his lips. 'I've come to help you build your snowman.'

Lexi giggles, skipping to his side to hold his hand. She seems far too happy to have his company to question why he's undercover.

Lexi and Jisung race to an empty space between competing families. By the time I've caught up, they are lying in the snow, laughing and firing snowballs at each other. I love seeing Jisung letting loose and being himself. Even out of character, he has a natural way with kids, and it's clear the two of them adore each other. When they notice me approaching, they both sit up quickly as if they have to behave in front of me. I laugh at their feigned innocence and catch them off guard by pelting them with snow.

My teammates retaliate with a barrage of snowballs, but luckily the elves save me from looking like their competition entry. Megaphone Elf announces we have one hour to build a snowman as the elves parade among us with backflips and terrible trombone playing.

In a relaxed mood, the three of us tumble around, gathering a snow pile. We roll three enormous balls; then Jisung and I balance them on top of each other. Pretty soon, our lopsided snowman starts taking shape.

While Lexi runs off to collect our accessories, Jisung blocks me against the back of our wintry work of art, wiggling his eyebrows. 'How about a kiss against a snowman?'

I gasp and immediately check that no one can see us. He gives me a quick peck on the nose, chuckling as he moves aside just as Lexi returns with a handful of buttons and a carrot.

As we finish building our *leaning tower of snowman*, we notice everyone around us is taking the competition far more seriously, meticulously crafting their snowmen with intricate details. But we've been focused on having fun together rather than winning. And it shows.

'What shall we do to make our snowman extra special, Lex?'

After a moment of thinking, Lexi falls to her knees and scoops up some snow. 'Prince… Man, please could you help me make a snow dog?'

Jisung joins her, and they start to mould the soft snow. 'Good plan, Lexi. What should we name him?'

'Barney.' She squeals at her idea. 'He can be a Snow Barney.'

I look up from their sculpture as an elf cartwheels past, giving me an idea. 'Ooh, I've got something too.' I hurry to move our snowman's face from the top to the bottom ball of snow. 'Look! He's upside down.' I chuckle, repositioning his stick arms. 'Now he looks like he's standing on his head, about to topple over.'

'Yay! I love him.' Lexi giggles and claps her hands, then gives Snow Barney some button eyes and a nose.

As we all stand back to appreciate our efforts, a red elf nose appears over my shoulder. 'Wow, what fun!' He giggles at our creation. 'This is what snowman-building is all about. Fun, fun, fun!'

Lexi's face is a picture as he skips away, and the three of us high-five each other. I pull her close for a hug and reach out to Jisung to join us, but he's looking over at the family next to us who are struggling to build their snowman. The dad's voice is rising in frustration, and his two young children are on the verge of tears.

'Ten more minutes!' Megaphone Elf announces, accompanied by another ear-splitting trombone screech.

Jisung puts his hand on my shoulder, about to speak, when Lexi taps us both. 'Can we go and help them?'

'Great minds, Lexi. I was just about to suggest that. Let's go.'

Jisung takes her hand, and we jog over to lend our assistance. The dad looks surprised but grateful. And ready for a lie down alone in a dark, quiet room, but still…

As Jisung helps the dad shape the snowman, I give him a hat and scarf, and Lexi helps the little ones add the buttons. Their faces light up as we work together, and they chat away merrily.

Between us all, we finish their snowman just in time. He may not be the most perfect one, but he was made full of heart and teamwork. The dad shakes Jisung by the hand. 'Cheers, mate. Really appreciate your help.' He ruffles his children's hair. 'It's tough keeping these two out of trouble. Don't know how the wife does it every day.' He looks worn out. I hope his wife is enjoying a lovely, well-earned massage in the spa.

'Time's up!' Megaphone Elf calls out, and the elf judges skip through all the snowmen, making their exaggerated expressions and randomly tossing confetti over the kids.

Lexi holds the little children's hands as the elves arrive, each of them wide-eyed and nervous. I seize the opportunity to hold Jisung's hand too. Trombone Elf throws confetti over the children, filling the air with colourful flakes and making them burst into giggles.

Jisung spins around, his face alight with laughter. A soft sigh escapes me at how carefree he looks, even though his face covering has slipped down. I find myself lost in his smile as the elves skip to the next family, leaving a trail of magic behind them.

When the snowmen have all been judged, the elves gather the children into a group. Megaphone Elf praises all their efforts and calls for a drumroll. 'And the winner is… the snowman with the green scarf over there.' The kids give a round of applause, followed by squeals of delight as small gifts are thrown into the crowd so everyone gets a prize. 'And… if you got covered in confetti, you also get a special prize.'

Lexi and the little ones run back to us waving their golden envelopes. 'Mum… Man, look! I got two!' Lexi squeals with joy, handing them to me one at a time. 'This one was for our snow dog, and this was for Christmas spirit.' She jumps around, hugging us all, beaming at our congratulations.

Jisung hugs me from behind, chuckling at the children's excitement.

'I wonder if these prizes are rigged in our favour?' I ask, with a sneaking suspicion Diane has had some input.

'Hey! Our snow dog's awesome!' He squeezes me, laughing. 'And anyway, they wouldn't have known Lexi would offer to help these guys.'

'Yeah, you're right.' I fight the urge to turn and kiss him. 'I've loved us playing together. You're good with your hands.' I turn around and give him a cheeky grin.

He winks back, turning my knees to jelly. 'Just wait and see what these hands have planned for you.' He's such a tease, and I love it. I can't wait to get him alone.

Lexi kicks the snow as she walks back towards us with a pouty face. She dramatically flops into my arms. 'The elf said there are no more competitions today.'

'How about we go for hot chocolate? Piggyback?'

She looks up at Jisung with her full excited smile back in place. 'Yay! Then we can see what we've won!'

FRIDAY

Up, Up, and Away

Lexi, Jisung, and I watch in fascination as the hot-air balloon inflates before us, its bright red fabric coming to life against the backdrop of white snowy meadow and clear blue sky. The sight is attracting quite a crowd, and Lexi is leaping around in excitement, encouraged by the pesky elves who have come to see us off.

'I can't believe I'm actually going to cross something off my bucket list.' I grab hold of Jisung's arm, squeezing my shoulders up around my ears, my skin prickling with goosebumps.

To any interested onlookers, it will just seem that our prize includes Prince Charming's company, and I'm sure it would be perfectly acceptable for him to help steady my nerves.

Jisung pulls my hand into his pocket, squeezing a little tighter than usual. He's been pretty quiet; I think he must be overcome with awe. It's not every day people get to experience anything so incredible. And I'm sure holding hands inside his pocket could be part of his supportive princely duties.

A sudden boost of loud whooshing from the hot air blowing in the balloon has Lexi running to my side.

'The fire's burning my face,' she whines, moving behind me. 'When will it be ready?'

'I don't think it will be long. Look, the basket has started to sway; it wants to float up already.'

Jisung's grip tightens around my fingers. Lexi hasn't noticed my missing hand. I can tell she's on the brink of saying she's bored. How quickly silly elves and the flurry of set-up crew action becomes dull.

'The balloon looks the same shape as your tattoo, doesn't it, Mum?' She fusses with the back of my coat, trying to lift it up.

I swat her away. 'It's cold, Lex. Don't pull my layers up so I've got bare skin showing. I'll freeze.'

Jisung holds out his hand. 'Come, Lexi. Let's meet the pilot.'

'Are we going on a plane as well?' she asks, skipping around his feet.

I shake my head, laughing, and follow them over to introduce ourselves to the pilot and a young couple who are also prize-winners.

'Mr Pilot…' Lexi wastes no time before jumping in with her questions. 'Am I old enough to go on the balloon ride?'

'Of course! You must be, what, sixteen? Seventeen?' he jokes.

'Nine, silly.' She giggles, looking chuffed to bits that someone has mistaken her for a teenager. 'Mr Pilot, how will we fly if the balloon hasn't got wings?'

With a twinkle in his eye, the pilot replies, 'Magic!'

***

Soon, the balloon is fully inflated and ready for us to climb aboard. Jisung lifts Lexi into the huge basket, but when he attempts to lift me, my legs are quivering and I need an extra hand from one of the crew. The other couple climbs into the basket on the opposite side, and then Jisung hops in with ease.

He stands in the corner of the basket, and I put my arm around him to steady my jelly legs. Lexi tucks herself in between us and zips her mouth shut for a couple of minutes as the pilot gives us a brief safety talk.

My smile is plastered to my face. I've wanted to do this for so long; it's another dream come true. Yet Jisung seems hesitant, and where he's clutching to the side of the basket, his knuckles have gone white. I put both my arms around his waist, my equivalent of a bear hug, and whisper, 'I've got you.' He kisses the top of my head and manages his first smile in quite some time.

As we launch gracefully up into the sky, I feel a rush of adrenaline and am overcome with emotion. Jisung grips my shoulder, and while Lexi cheers and waves down to the elves, I hold on tight to his rigid body.

As we ascend higher and higher, moving in the direction of the wind, the view of the landscape below becomes more and more breathtaking. The sun is setting, casting a warm, golden glow over the mountains in the distance, and rolling, snow-covered hills and forests stretch out as far as the eye can see. I gaze out across the sky, painted with hues of pink, orange, and purple, a little teary-eyed at the sense of wonder and awe at the beauty below us.

The basket feels secure under foot, even with its gentle creaking sounds, and slowly Jisung's grip on both me and the basket loosens.

'How are you doing?'

'I didn't expect to be nervous. I'm fine with flying.' I'm so pleased to see his smile return. He turns to face outwards, captivated by the view. I still don't take my arms from around my courageous prince, and I realise I'm looking more at his face than at the view. He meets my gaze with a warm smile and a big hug. 'There's nowhere I'd rather be.'

As we soar through the sky, the chilly air only adds to the thrill. The sound of the flame is a soft roar, and the heat from the balloon surrounds us, bringing a sense of comfort and security. Jisung's hand clasps mine and I rest my head against him, so grateful we are together to marvel at the vastness of the world around us.

Lexi remains wide-eyed and enthralled, bouncing with excitement as she points out landmarks and wildlife below. I love seeing her so full of joy, and it brings a smile to my face every time she gasps with wonder. Although, I do have to keep reminding her not to jump too high – knowing my luck, she's inherited my mishap tendencies and could fall right through the basket.

When the pilot pulls out thermos flasks, Lexi sees her cue to ask if the balloon really works by magic. As he pours her a hot chocolate, he explains in Lexi-friendly language the mixture of magic and science. He patiently answers all of Lexi's curious questions as he passes mugs to Jisung and I. The hot, buttered, spiced rum certainly heats our insides and eases the numbness of our cold toes.

'How is the balloon hanging in the air? Are we floating on a cloud? What if we crash into a cloud? Will we go up into space? Will we have to parachute down to Earth?'

As the sun begins to dip below the horizon, the sky turns to a deep shade of purple. The world below looks magical, like a fairy tale come to life, and contentment washes over me. Sharing this moment with Jisung and Lexi is a memory of pure happiness that I'll treasure forever.

When the balloon begins its descent towards the ground, Lexi wraps her arms around us, bringing us together in a warm group hug. She's been perfectly accepting of Jisung and me being physically close, as long as she's included and in the centre.

Lexi looks up with a pout. 'I want to stay in the sky forever.'

'Perhaps Santa could turn you into a bird?' Jisung chuckles and pats her head.

'The hour's gone too quickly, hasn't it?' I'm not keen to return to the ground rules of keeping my distance from Jisung either.

Lexi giggles and wrinkles her nose. 'You two smell like you've got fire coming out of your mouths.' Then she adds with a mischievous grin, 'I bet you could inflate the balloon with your rum dragon breath!' She makes us both laugh, and I give her a swift tickle. Cheeky little monkey.

The mountains and forests below us seem closer, and the distant town is growing larger by the second. The heat from the balloon fades away, and the air grows colder as we approach the ground. The pilot points out the ground crew, who have been following us with the trailer and two executive cars.

'Where's the palace?' Lexi searches all around, looking puzzled. 'Are we lost?'

The pilot laughs fondly at Lexi's concerned little face and throws her a chocolate truffle, which seems to instantly ease her worries. I think she's made his trip more entertaining too.

We brace ourselves for landing, and as we touch down gently on the ground, we're all on a high, exhilarated by our adventure of a lifetime.

Back on the ground, the crew are waiting with champagne and a table full of mouth-watering sweet delicacies. Lexi can't stop talking about all the incredible things she saw from up high, and Jisung shares his favourite moments, already seeming to have forgotten his nervousness at the start. I squeeze his hand, proud of his bravery.

We toast the quiet couple, who are celebrating their sixth anniversary, which feels like the perfect ending of our incredible experience. Until the young woman asks Jisung and I, 'How long have you two been together?'

Jisung coughs. Speechless, I stare at the ground, panicking about what Lexi's reaction will be, and also slightly curious about what Jisung may say. But my wonderful, bubbly daughter, who usually says the most embarrassing thing at such times, jumps in with, 'I'm going on a princess sleepover tonight!'

The conversation swiftly changes to her second prize, and Jisung and I share a look of *That was awkward*.

'Sorry I can't come to the honeymoon with you, Mum, but I'm busy tonight.'

'I'll be just fine, Lex. We'll go back to the hotel and pack, and you go and have fun.'

I peek up at Jisung, who glances back with the naughtiest twinkle in his eye.

***

As I push open the door to the 'Crown' honeymoon suite, my heart is racing; I can't believe I get to spend a whole night here with Jisung. I step inside with a gasp, immediately struck by its grandeur. The ceilings are high, the furnishings are ornate, and the room is unlike anything I have ever seen before.

'Jisung?'

There's no reply, just soft, relaxing music. I didn't expect him to be here yet, but I couldn't wait to come up after dropping an extremely excited Lexi off for her sleepover.

My feet sink into the plush carpet as I spin around, taking in every inch of our fantastical suite. Shimmering fabrics drape the ceiling and intricate gold-leaf crown designs adorn the walls, catching the light and sparkling like jewels. The king-sized bed is covered in rose petals that are scattered in a heart shape, and the sweet aroma of fresh flowers fills the air.

The couch by the fireplace looks so cosy and inviting that I sink into it, snuggling into the furry throw draped over the back. The flickering light from the flames casts a warm glow on the nearby coffee table, which is laden with a platter of delicious-looking fruits and pastries.

I yawn long and hard. It's already been a long day, and the warmth of the fire is making me sleepy. Hiding behind a vase of flowers, I spy a cafetiere on the table. Oh, Fairy-Tale Wonderland! You think of everything. I love you! Thank you, naughty elves. A night with Prince Charming is the best prize ever! I chuckle to myself, feeling like royalty, pampered and indulged in every way.

I down two cups of emergency caffeine and jump up, eager to get ready before Jisung arrives. My gaze falls on the large jacuzzi in the corner of the room, the water illuminated with coloured lights. I can't wait to soak in its soothing bubbles, and maybe have another steamy snuggle later, but right now I need speed.

I wander into the bathroom and have to stop and just stare to take it all in. It's as spacious as the bedroom, and its sleek modern design is stunning. A massive round bathtub full of rose petals is in the centre, surrounded by softly glowing lanterns and with champagne at the side. The amount of products on display around the double sink makes it look like a boutique parfumerie in a fluffy-white-towel shop. I'm in bathroom heaven.

Stripping off, I head to the state-of-the-art walk-in rain shower at the far end of the room, looking forward to my body being caressed by warm, gentle summer rain. I step into the shower area that has no door – how strange! But at least I won't be attacked by a cold, wet shower curtain like at Mother's. The shower head above is a huge, green-glowing rectangle, and the number of knobs on the wall is mind-boggling.

I turn the first knob and hope for the best. Ahhh. I stand under the warm spray and close my eyes, visualising memories of Lexi jumping through the sprinklers at the park on a sunny afternoon. The tingle on my skin is like a fingertip massage all over. Although, it would take a couple of hours to wash my hair in this light drizzle, so I fiddle with the controls. The glow changes to blue, then purple, and then soft music plays. I fiddle some more.

'Monsoon!' I splutter through the torrential downpour, still trying to find a happy medium.

Finally, I manage to get the temperature and flow just right, and select one of the delicious-smelling shampoos to squirt into my hair. A sudden short blast of freezing water hits my backside from somewhere on the wall, making my breath catch.

More. Icy. Blasts.

I let out a yelp with each blast and scramble to adjust the controls, trying to change the setting to just nice, not nice with hits of snowball.

Eventually, I find a balance, and the shower manages to restore my trust.

***

I dance around the bathroom in my warmed robe, drying my hair while testing all the fragrances, trying to find the perfect one to match the mood of the evening. I'm drawn to a sweet, woodsy scent that reminds me of Jisung's natural aroma, then select the fanciest bottle and spray in the hope of intoxicating him when I get him all to myself.

I move on to peruse the vast array of skincare products, finding a rejuvenating face mask and smoothing it on, enjoying the cool, refreshing sensation. I slather on silky creams and sweet-smelling body butters, relishing the time to pamper myself with luxurious items I would never splurge on for myself.

The knock on the door makes my heart stop – he can't be here already! Inwardly screaming, I grab a towel and rub my face clear of the white, dried-on face mask, and spin around realising there's no time to get dressed, let alone do my make-up. I rush to the door and take a moment to breathe.

There he is, standing in the doorway looking utterly gorgeous in a sharp, dark suit that highlights his broad shoulders. His playful smirk makes my knees weak. I cross my arms over my bathrobe, cheeks flaming. When I imagined this moment, I silently took Jisung by the hand and led him inside straight to the bed, being all sexy-like. However, in reality, Jisung takes in my state of undress and laughs.

'You naked already, Cally? You're not going to wine and dine me first?'

I look down self-consciously. 'No, no, I didn't mean... I ran out of–' Jisung's lips pause my rambling. I stumble backwards as he walks me back inside the room and presses me against the wall.

With a gentle caress of my neck, he whispers, 'That's fine by me.'

My heart pounds as he loosens my belt and presses his fully clothed body against my skin, his lips brushing across my shoulder. My breathing is fast, the sensation exhilarating. I want to tear at his clothes to feel his skin against mine, but he pins my arms to the wall, leaving me defenceless against his slow, lingering kisses.

A knock at the door has us both cursing through panting breaths.

'I'll get it. You cover up in the bathroom.' Jisung plants a quick kiss on my cheek as he adjusts his trousers and straightens his jacket.

While my breathing returns to a more human rate, I do the speediest make-up application ever known while spraying more perfume and hopping around putting on my underwear. So classy. I would roll my eyes at myself if I had time.

Jisung taps on the bathroom door. 'Can I come in?'

'Of course. Come and check this room out.'

Jisung pokes his head around the door and doesn't take his eyes from mine, oblivious to the incredible features around me.

'It was room service. Dinner has arrived, but don't rush.' He dips his eyes, and as he opens the door wider, I see the long silver garment bag. 'I hope you don't mind, but I thought you might like a royal dress to match our royal room.' Chewing on his lip, he looks up, and I step towards him, wrapping my arms around his strong frame, burying my face in his chest and inhaling the scent of his cologne. 'I don't deserve you; you're too wonderful.'

'I don't deserve you! But here we are.' He chuckles and kisses my forehead. 'You don't have to wear it. If you don't like it or you want something different, I'll get it changed for you.' His tone is gentle and cautious, as though he doesn't want to offend me.

I stare up at him in disbelief. It hadn't even occurred to me to dress up; not for one moment did I ever imagine this.

'You're so thoughtful, thank you.' There go those fireworks exploding inside me again. I don't even know how to express how he makes me feel or how I feel about him. All I can do is squeeze him.

'Call me if you need anything. I'll fix us some drinks.' Jisung kisses my cheek and leaves me to get dressed.

Unzipping the bag, I pray the dress will fit over my curves. I don't mind what it is; the fact he's chosen it specially for me already makes me feel like a princess.

An ethereal, silvery grey shimmers from inside, and I pull off the bag to reveal a light and flowy floor-length gown with an embroidered boat-neck top. It's elegant and sophisticated and absolutely perfect.

I'm beyond excited to step into the soft materials and slip on the three-quarter-length sleeves. My arms aren't stretchy enough to pull up the zip at the back, but it fits beautifully. I wouldn't be surprised if the hotel shop keeps a record of guest sizes for times like this. Before I head out for Jisung's assistance, I take a last look in the mirror, and I love what I see.

Standing by the illuminated bottles neatly lined at the mini bar, he turns as I approach him, his eyes shining as I spin around. 'Please could you zip me up, my Prince Charming?'

'Anything for you, my princess.'

I hold up my hair and he slowly slides the zip while kissing my neck. I wish I wasn't starving so we could skip dinner and I could go straight to my Jisung dessert.

He finishes with a tickly, growly bite on the side of my neck, making me giggle as he takes my hand and twirls me. Catching me in his arms, with a long, passionate smooch, he murmurs, 'I'm the luckiest man in the world to have you in my arms tonight.' It blows my mind this angel feels that way about me too.

As Jisung hands me a chilled flute of champagne, his admiring look gives my confidence a boost. The feel of his hand resting gently on my back makes me stand taller in the striking dress he chose. He guides me to our intimate table for two, where the view from the floor-to-ceiling windows takes my breath away: a pristine blanket of snow glistening in the moonlight with a sea of twinkling lights stretching far into the distance. As we take in the magical moment together, the world outside fades away, replaced by the warmth of our connection and the appetising gourmet meal waiting for us.

Jisung pulls out my chair before sitting across from me. I smooth my dress under the table, pulse quickening as I'm hit by sudden nerves at our first formal date. But I'm immediately transfixed by the heart-shaped platters under the soft candlelight, rose petals scattered around.

'I'll have this one.' I laugh, pointing to the indulgent love-heart fruits and dark-chocolate-dipping extravaganza scattered with edible flowers.

'What do you think – Turkish? Lebanese?' He peers closely at the mezze of tender meats, vibrant vegetables, and dips, all strewn with dried rose petals and pomegranate seeds.

'Not sure, but it smells amazing and looks so pretty.' Lunchtime seems long ago, and my stomach is about to make some thunderous rumbling. 'Where do we start?'

Jisung rubs his hands together in anticipation of a feast. 'Just dive right in.' He goes straight for the chicken skewers and, with each selection he makes, offers to place some on my plate first. We begin to eat and chat, enjoying each other's company and the moreish food.

'So was your hot-air-balloon ride everything you hoped it would be?' he asks, reaching across the table for my hand.

'The whole day feels like a dream come true.' A warmth spreads through me, and my heart races as I think of all the fun we've had. 'Apart from when Lexi was born, I think this has been the best day of my entire life.'

Jisung bows his head. 'I am honoured to have spent it with you.'

I stroke his fingers. He always knows the right thing to say to make my heart melt. 'Who knows? Maybe our next adventure will be even more incredible than this one.'

'Hold up!' His grin becomes mischievous. 'The day's not over yet, and tonight is going to be legendary.' He gives me an exaggerated wink and we both laugh, although he does make a fair point...

'What daredevil experience are you going to scare me to death with next time? Base jumping from the Empire State Building? Free falling from space?'

'How about we go down next time?' I tease. 'Swimming with sharks, maybe?'

He rubs the back of his neck, looking out of the window. 'Yeah, whatever you say, babe.'

I laugh, then turn serious. 'Just so we're all clear, that was a joke. I really, really don't want any surprise diving dates.' I pause, then add, 'And I certainly don't want to struggle in, or out, of a wetsuit.' I shiver imagining the unflattering neoprene stuck to my body. No thanks!

He laughs at me and pours some more drinks. 'Are you ready to move on to dessert?'

'Ooh yes! I've saved some room.' I pat my stomach, eyeing the goodies on our second platter. 'Look! Fortune cookies!' I hand one to Jisung. 'You go first.'

He snaps his open and pulls out the strip of paper. 'As you share this delicious meal, savour every moment together, and enjoy each other for dessert.'

'What?' I laugh incredulously. 'It doesn't say that.'

'It does, look!' He waves the little piece of paper out of my reach, laughing. 'Oh, OK. I might have added a couple of words at the end.'

My eyebrow flicks up. 'Not a bad idea, though.'

Jisung immediately pushes his chair back, looking as if he's about to pounce, which makes me squeal and run. He chases me for all of two steps before catching me and smothering me in tickly kisses while I giggle and squirm. I manage to free my arms and place my hands on the back of his neck. Pulling him down towards me, I whisper in his ear, 'I need chocolate.'

Back in my seat, I snap my fortune cookie and read aloud, 'Together, you have the perfect recipe for a lifetime of happiness.' My heart skips as I look up to meet Jisung's gaze, the candles bathing his smiling face in their delicate fluttering flames.

'Awww,' we say in unison as we dip heart-shaped fruits in chocolate to feed each other. Dessert is as delicious as it looks, but a sense of dread creeps into my mind, and I don't enjoy it as much as I want to.

As we finish our meal, I take a deep breath, knowing that I need to bring up the elephant my stupid fortune cookie brought into the room.

'Jisung,' I begin tentatively, 'we need to talk, and I don't know how to bring it up.'

He looks at me with concern, his hand reaching out to gently squeeze mine. 'What's on your mind, Cally?'

I fidget with the napkin in my lap, twisting it around my fingers as I search for the right words. 'I'm scared about what happens next, for us.' I drop the napkin and cup his hand in mine, drawing strength from his touch. 'I don't want to lose you again, but I can't help worrying about how far apart we live, and I don't know how we'll...' My heart thumps painfully in my chest at the thought of being without him, my eyes stinging with the threat of tears.

Jisung nods, his expression serious. 'It's been on my mind too.'

'I know it has.' I reach out and stroke his cheek, searching for a glimmer of hope in his eyes. 'I just can't imagine how we can maintain a relationship from such a distance.'

Jisung takes both my hands in his, his grip firm and reassuring. 'I understand your worries, Cally. But I don't want to let the distance keep us from exploring what we have. We can work through this and figure out a way to make it work.'

A tiny bud of hope begins to form in my heart. 'What do you suggest we do?'

Jisung smiles, his warmth infectious. He stands and leads me to the couch, pulling me onto his lap so we can face this together. 'Let's take it one day at a time. We can talk regularly, visit each other when we can, and make the most of the time we do have together. Who knows? Maybe one day we'll find a way to be closer to each other.'

I feel some sense of relief wash over me at his words, my tense muscles relaxing slightly, but the worries remain. 'I have to consider Lexi first, and we both have so much work. I don't want to put too much pressure on you to visit me all the time.'

Jisung nods. 'It won't be easy, but I'm willing to do whatever it takes to make this work. I don't want to lose you either, Cally.'

I wrap my arms around him, closing my eyes and letting myself be comforted by his embrace. The fear is very real. I've seen how badly I coped when I lost him in the summer. 'I'm just feeling a bit hopeless about it all. It feels like there are so many obstacles in the way.'

Jisung's expression is understanding and assured, his unwavering gaze fixed on me. 'I'm not giving up on you. I'm not giving up on us – we'll get through this together. We just need to keep talking and be open with each other.'

His words make my heart swell, tears pricking my eyes at his commitment.

We sit by the fire for some time, holding each other, comforting each other. I'm grateful to have Jisung by my side, willing to work through difficulties with me and find a way to make our relationship work. 'I'm sorry I've ruined our evening.'

'Cally, my love, we're stronger now we've talked things through. No evening could be ruined when I have you in my arms.' Our kiss is long, slow, and deliciously chocolatey.

I excuse myself to freshen up in the bathroom. I need to perk up our evening, and I think I know how, but I'm the most nervous I've ever been.

I take out the bag and stare at it for a while. I still don't know if I have the guts to go through with this crazy plan. I don't know what possessed me to buy it in the first place, other than that the model looked stunning. *Badass Cally, you better show up pretty quick before Jisung thinks I've fallen down the plug hole.*

I'm going to have to go with a different tactic; I just can't do sultry and seductive. But I can do playful and laugh at myself, and I think Jisung will appreciate that.

I slip the black fabric from the bag and run my fingers over its silky texture. Up-for-fun Cally mode on, I quickly change into the new lingerie before I get cold feet.

The bodysuit itself is beautiful and sexy and feels soft against my skin. I find myself standing taller as I check it covers everything it's supposed to. I brave a quick glance in the mirror and I love it. It's so special and perfect for the occasion. I tie the large, flirty bow around the front of the bust, a bit more confident now my boobs have some coverage. With a deep breath, I shake out my hair and head back to Jisung.

My heart races as I turn the corner and peek out to see Jisung lounging on the furry rug by the fire. He looks up and his mouth falls open as he spots me shyly stepping into full view. I try to keep my voice steady. 'Jisung, I have a present for you.'

He gets up to his knees, holding his arms out to me, the desire in his eyes making my nerves melt away. 'You are the best present ever.' His voice is eager and filled with admiration. 'Come, let me unwrap you.'

SATURDAY

Slush

Jisung stirs beside me, his sleepy eyes blinking open, and he wraps his arms around me, pulling me closer. The sheets rustle as I snuggle into his embrace, feeling the warmth of his body against mine. His touch is gentle and reassuring, and contentment settles over me. This is the way to start the day: no rushing, no walk of shame, just us relishing the peacefulness of the moment.

'Good morning, beautiful.' Jisung's voice is husky with sleep, and he looks even more gorgeous than usual with his dark hair tousled. 'Room service came a little while ago. I didn't want to wake you.' He props himself up on his elbow and strokes back my hair, and I feel a rush of affection for him.

I stretch my arms above my head and prop myself against the pillows. 'I thought I was imagining the smell of coffee.' I reach for the steaming mug on the nightstand. 'Mmm... Imagine waking up like this every morning.'

Jisung takes a sip of his coffee, and after I check the time, we lounge in bed with his head resting on my chest, enjoying the stillness.

Last night only intensified my feelings for this tender, passionate man. He is all my dreams come true, wrapped up in one perfect, delicious package. I want to fling open the windows and sing a princess-movie-style official announcement to the world – *My heart belongs to Jisung!*

When I put down my mug, he reaches up to kiss me, his lips warm and tender, the taste of coffee lingering on our tongues, and I wrap my arms around his neck, deepening the kiss.

He looks into my eyes, making my chest flutter with excitement. My eyebrow flicks upwards, his eyes narrow, and a mischievous grin spreads across his face. My body tingles with anticipation as his head disappears under the duvet and he murmurs, 'Let's make the morning even better shall we?'

***

'Muuum, hurry up!'

Lexi's legs rub against mine every time they bounce under the table – she's ready to ping into action any second.

'I'm just finishing my coffee. I'll only be a couple of minutes.'

'Can't you drink any faster?'

'Go and get your boot–'

She leaps up and runs from the dining hall, calling out 'sorry' after bumping straight into Shana on her way out of the door. I go to stand to apologise again on Lexi's behalf and am surprised when she approaches my table. Shana chuckles. 'Someone's in a hurry!'

'Sorry, she's full of beans after her princess sleepover, and now she's desperate to go and see the reindeer outside.'

Shana's smile drops. 'I apologise for interrupting your plans, but Mrs Todgers would like to see you.'

'Oh.' My eyes flit to the door after Lexi, but she's long gone. 'Right now?'

'Yes, sorry. I've already arranged for Nanny Prim to meet Lexi.'

I'm gutted to have to miss magical reindeer time with my little girl. But Shana looks and sounds serious, and it makes my stomach twist in knots.

Shana hovers, waiting to accompany me to Diane's office. I leave my coffee and trail behind her. Has Diane heard Jisung and I were together last night? Or am I being summoned because she's read my ideas and cancelling my assignment? Either way, I'm terrified. I hate dealing with conflict and confrontations. And I'm exhausted, which doesn't help matters.

I knock on Diane's door with a trembling hand. A muffled 'Come in' sounds from inside. I take a deep breath and open the door. Diane's on the phone and gestures for me to enter. She points to the coffee ready on the table and to the couch. I do as I'm told – pour myself a coffee, take the cup over to the couch, and sit down. The wait is torment; my mind has time to visit horrible places.

I overhear Diane bringing her conversation to a close and prepare myself. I grip my knees, bracing for the worst. The moment she says goodbye and presses the button to end the call, I spring to my feet, sending coffee flying down my trouser leg. 'Please don't send us home on Christmas Eve.' I stare at her with pleading eyes while she stares back for a few moments that feel like hours, her face crinkled in... bewilderment?

'Whatever do you mean, Cally?' She frowns as she walks over to the couch and puts her hand on my shoulder before we sit down together. I cough and wipe my hot leg. I don't want to give her reasons to send me home, so I look down, stay quiet, and wait for her to speak.

'I've read through Shana's notes from your meeting.' She pauses to drink some of her coffee, allowing my body the time to slump in anticipation. I know I haven't finished my work yet and time is rapidly running out. I don't think I can dig myself out of this hole, so I await my fate. I steal a glance at her – she's still frowning at me.

'Is everything all right, my dear? I'm sorry to call you away from your daughter, but I do need to talk to you.'

I swallow hard and sit up straight to look at her. 'I'll be OK. Just hit me with it.'

'Sorry, I'll get straight to the point.' Her face softens. 'I need you, Cally.'

'Huh?' I accidentally interrupt.

'You've seen that I'm a little overwhelmed with my new management responsibilities, and I feel you are the person I can trust to help.'

I nod. 'Of course, I'll help in any way I can.' I perk up a little bit; she doesn't sound cross.

'Your ideas for the resort show me that you understand our ethos and the direction we are going in this new phase.'

I nod slowly. I have no idea where she is going with this or why she sounds hesitant.

'I have a proposition. I know it's not ideal in your circumstances; there are some solutions we can offer, and you need time to digest and make your decision, but I understand if you decide it's not right for you.' She stops talking as though she has made sense and looks at me as if waiting for a response. I frown. Did I miss something?

'Sorry, Diane, I don't really understand.'

About to take a sip of coffee, she stops before the cup reaches her mouth, and puts it on the table. 'Oh yes, the proposition.' She takes a deep breath. I gulp.

'I would like you to come and work here, with me, as my management assistant.'

I respond with a coffee-spluttering 'What?'

'Your ideas for the children's club and character books are inspired, along with your vision for extra revenue streams and the marketing. With Frank taking a step back, I think you would be a wonderful asset to both the resort and to me personally.'

Gob. Smacked.

I stare at Diane with my mouth open before shaking my head, unable to believe the words she has spoken. I cough, blinking rapidly, trying to get my brain to catch up. 'That would mean… moving here, would it?'

'It would, yes. I know that might be difficult for you with your daughter, and that's half the reason I hesitate to ask. Of course, we can offer accommodation for you both as part of the package.' She smiles, but with concern in her eyes.

'And the other half of the reason for hesitating?' I daren't get my hopes up before I have the full details – so far this sounds too perfect.

Diane takes another moment to pause. 'The development plans for the resort may take some time, and while there would initially be a lot of work to get things moving…' She pauses again. Meanwhile, I hold my breath waiting for the *but…*

'The role I am offering would only be part time. And I know that may cause some financial compromises.'

I let out a rush of breath that I've been holding and hurl my arms around Diane, making her jump and laugh.

'Thank you,' I manage to whisper. My mind is spinning with all the details that need to be considered, but right now, I am fit to burst. I'm still hugging her – I need her to keep me grounded so I don't float up and away like a helium balloon.

When I fall against the back of the couch, I am still speechless. Diane fills my silence with details and role responsibilities that flow straight over my head. I feel faint. The implications of this offer are immense.

'You look a little pale, Cally. Let's leave it here and you go and get some fresh air.' Diane stands and takes my cup. 'I'm sorry to land this on you so close to Christmas when you're busy having fun. Take all the time you need to think it over.'

I stand and grip Diane's hand. I think I manage a smile, and the only words I can utter are 'Thank you'.

***

The top of the outdoor staircase at the Palace Hotel's entrance provides a vantage point of the village green, which is now white and strewn with colours. It resembles the ending scene of a movie where the whole town is gathered and full of festive cheer to power Santa's sleigh. Families are playing in the snow, all the staff are dressed in bright green-and-red elf costumes, lights are twinkling, and people are singing carols accompanied by a brass band. There's more Christmas spirit here than all my previous Christmases combined. Down in front, children are petting the visiting reindeer, and that's where I expect I'll find Lexi.

I zig-zag my way through the cheery crowds and decorated trees. The atmosphere is all-encompassing, which gives my brain a welcome rest from thinking. Lexi's easy to spot in her bright pink hat, and I stop to watch her for a moment before I go over to meet her.

She is rubbing the nose of a reindeer while feeding him a carrot, and her smile is merry and bright. She's radiating a joy that melts my mummy heart. This is the Christmas she deserves – a time of making magical childhood memories that she will treasure forever.

Standing behind Lexi is Nanny P, who looks equally happy – the kind of supportive and loving grown-up that Lexi needs in her life. Not a grumpy old dad who ignores her in favour of a trollop in the kitchen. This could be our reality if we moved here. I shake my head; it seems unbelievable.

A team of elves lead a convoy of reindeer with jingling bells, pulling shiny green sleighs. As I reach Lexi, she is jumping with excitement, ready for a sleigh ride through the snowy resort grounds. She jumps into my arms when she sees me.

'Mum! Come and meet Crystal!' She takes my hand and drags me over to the reindeer. I pat Crystal's back and ruffle her mane. 'Awww, she's beautiful.' I'm not sure how much more happiness my heart can take as I scratch behind Crystal's ears.

'Nanny P is taking me for a sleigh ride!' Lexi's smile fades. 'There's only room for two people...' She pouts. 'Do you mind, Mum? I can go again with you afterwards, if you want?'

My heart sinks. As much as I want to share this with her, work calls. I put my arms around her and kiss her head. 'It's OK, my darling. Go and have fun. I need to do a bit more work anyway.'

'But it's Christmas Eve!' Lexi's voice is tinged with sadness.

'I know, sweetheart.' I stroke her cold little cheek, forcing brightness into my tone. 'But it's my work that meant we were lucky enough to come here – and it means you're lucky enough to play with Nanny P.'

Lexi takes hold of Nanny P's hand, and they beam at each other. She suddenly looks back at me, eyebrows knitted together. 'Mum, will I have time to get a ballgown?'

'Of course!' Excitement bubbles up inside me at the thought of sharing this mother-daughter experience. I pull her hat down to cover her ears. 'We'll go this afternoon, and you can choose the perfect dress.'

'Yay!' Lexi dances on the spot, unable to keep still for more than a minute.

'Prince Charming,' Lexi calls out behind me, 'will you dance with me at the ball this evening?'

I spin around to see him join us, and feel my face flush.

'With my best dance partner? You bet!' He flashes his dazzling smile and dimpled cheeks, and Lexi crinkles her nose and squeals. My whole being wants to snuggle into his arms and give him a million kisses.

'And how are my favourite ladies?' He puts his arms around me and Lexi. I lean into his subtle embrace, desperate to wrap my arms around him.

'We're going on a sleigh ride!' Lexi's back to bouncing around, making us laugh with her enthusiasm. She's shaken off Jisung's arm, but he keeps his arm around me, making me feel warm and fuzzy. And a little nervous in case it's noticed, especially by Lexi, who wouldn't hesitate to comment. Loudly.

Nanny P gives me a knowing look. 'Shall we go now, Lexi?'

'Yes! Yes! Yes!' She grabs Nanny P's hand and sings, 'Bye!' as she pulls the impressively patient woman behind her.

Jisung turns to face me, covertly holding my hand by our sides. I look up into his eyes, trying hard not to swoon in public. But his eyes are dreamy, and I don't think anything could stop my face showing how he makes me feel.

'Can we go and get coffee?'

An 'Mmmm' escapes from my lips, and I break away from standing so close, trying to keep my swooning under control. He laughs as my hand covers my silly grinning face, while we walk.

We sit opposite each other at a table in the corner of the quaint little coffee shop. I quickly glance around to check who might see us, but there's only one other couple in here, and they're busy dealing with a toddler tantrum. Jisung raises his hand to attract the waitress and calls, 'Two whipped coffees, please.'

'My favourite, thank you.'

He winks. 'They taste almost as delicious as you.'

My eyes fly open wide. 'Shhhh!' Colour stings my cheeks, making him laugh. He links his fingers with mine across the table, which feels naughty, yet so nice.

'Are you sure we should be sitting together?' I whisper.

'It's fine, and anyway, I couldn't wait.'

We sit quietly for a short while, just looking into each other's eyes like soppy teenagers while he strokes my hand. Not appropriate public behaviour, although it would be much worse if my thoughts had their way. But I'm bursting to tell him my news and can't hold it in any longer. I take a deep breath. 'I have something to tell you.' At the same time, Jisung says, 'I've got great news.' We both laugh, and I nod for him to speak first.

'Do you remember I said I spoke to my agent when I was thinking of moving back to Korea?' He raises his eyebrows, and I nod back. 'Well, I've been offered the lead role in a new series,' he says with infectious passion.

'Oh my goodness, congratulations! That's fantastic!'

'Filming starts in the new year.' His eyes shine as he speaks.

As I take in his words, my smile wavers. 'You're... going back to... Korea?'

He nods. 'I can see my family.' His eyes redden and he blinks back his tears. Suddenly it hits me...

'You're leaving?' I freeze, staring into Jisung's eyes, desperate for this to stop and rewind as my dreams come crashing down in front of me. My bottom lip quivers as I try to speak. 'But... what about us? What about me?'

'Cally.' Jisung puts his hand over mine, but I pull my hand back. He reaches for me again but I recoil, the sting of betrayal too fresh.

'I've been trying to figure out how we can be together.' Now I'm blinking back tears. 'Everything was about to work out perfectly, but now you're leaving. *Leaving me.*' My pulse races, chest tightening as panic sets in. I start to shake as reality sinks in.

'Cally.'

I shake my head; I can't face him. My heart has shattered. I can't believe this is happening, that after everything, I'm about to lose him again.

'Cally,' he says in a louder voice. 'Stop. You're not listening to me.'

My body sinks in defeat. What more is there to say? He's leaving, end of story. I stare up at him and splutter, 'I was about to move here to be with you.' I'm struggling to stay calm, but it's too late. I slap my forehead. 'What was I thinking? I should have known this was too good to be true.'

'I don't want to hurt you, Cally. Don't you trust me?'

I dig my fingernails into the skin of my palms. 'Trust you? How can I when you're about to leave me? When I was falling in love with you?' My breath shudders, and tears stream down my face.

How can this be happening? I thought he wanted us to be together too, but obviously I was wrong. I'm such a deluded fool. I can't do this. I can't cope with my heart being broken again. But I can't beg him to stay.

I feel my shoulders sag as all hope seeps from my body. 'I give up.' I sigh, my words barely above a whisper.

'Cally?'

I can't raise my head to look at him. 'You may as well go... and take my dreams with you.' I take off the mushroom house bracelet and place it into his hand.

With a solemn expression, he scrapes back his chair and walks away. I stare after him, slack-jawed. How the hell did this just happen? I couldn't wait to tell him we could be together, and now I'm here alone.

He's left the coffee shop.

He's left me.

I stand, every fibre of me wanting to run after him, to make this stop... But my legs freeze in place, hurt and despair rooting me to the floor. What would I say? No words can fix this. I don't want him to give up his dreams for me. I slump back in my seat, dizzy and weak, and my head falls into my hands. He let go of me and walked away.

We're over.

It's all over.

With extra bad timing, the waitress brings over the coffees. 'Will Prince Charming be coming back?'

'No, he's gone.'

SATURDAY

The Most Wonderful Time of the Year

'Then I gave him back the bracelet.' My breath shudders as I try to get my words out. 'And then he left me.' Another outbreak of tears spills down my face. Thalia puts her arm around me and passes my drink. She knew the drill as soon as she saw my face when I walked past reception. She brought me to the small bar and ordered the drinks while I slumped at a table, and she barely said a word as I filled her in.

'Thank you for being my shoulder to cry on.' I dry my eyes with my palms and finally make eye contact. The shell-shocked expression on her face makes me laugh through my sobs. 'I'm sorry, was that a lot to take in all in one go?'

Thalia's eyes remain wide as she drains her drink, making me giggle again. She raises her hand to the barman and makes finger signals to order another round, then shakes her head as if trying to slot all the pieces of my story together.

'I have so many questions,' she says slowly.

I sit up straight and take a deep breath. 'You can ask. I trust you not to say anything.'

'Prince Charming?' she asks, her jaw dropping to her lap. I nod.

'And you were going to move here?'

'It was a big possibility.'

Her brow furrows. 'And you're sure he's going back to South Korea?'

I nod, tears refilling my eyes.

Thalia takes a big slurp of her fresh cocktail as it arrives at our table, and hesitates. 'Do you mind if I say something?'

I nod, feeling like I'm about to get a lecture, but about which part, I'm not sure.

'It's just… it sounds like he really likes you. Do you really think he would move away for good?' She puts her hand on mine, stopping me from ripping the paper drinks mat into any more tiny pieces. 'Could he just be going to work away for a short time?'

My eyes dart up to hers. 'But that's when everything went wrong with Ben.' My words gush out and hang in the air. I stare at the pile of confetti I've torn, puzzling my thoughts together.

'When Ben started working away from home, that's when he started to drift away. I never admitted it to myself. I thought it would be better to ignore the signs and pretend it wasn't happening.' I take a sip of my drink and fiddle with the straw. I'm strangely detached from my words; they feel very matter-of-fact. Any upset over losing Ben seems a distant memory; I checked out emotionally long before I left.

'I think I always knew he wasn't alone on those business trips. I can't go through that again.'

Thalia puts her arm around me like a shroud of calm. She rests her head against my shoulder. 'Jisung isn't Ben.'

I take a deep breath as those three words slowly sink in. My head droops like I've been both chastised and slapped with a reality check. I slump back on the table and lay my head in my hands. 'I've done it again, haven't I? I jumped to conclusions and didn't listen.'

It's too late now to recognise that my reaction to Jisung was clouded by my past. In that one split second, all the growth and progress I've made in the past few months was washed away by a flood of fear that he was going to abandon me.

I slowly sit up straight and sigh. 'I've really screwed up this time. I panicked and lashed out and overreacted. And he walked away and doesn't want anything to do with me.' I finish my first drink. 'I can't believe how many times I've been dumped, when we were only together for a couple of days.'

Thalia raises her eyebrow at me. I must be blathering again. 'What are you going to do now?'

I sigh. I'm pretty sure she won't let me get away with just shrugging my shoulders like a petulant child. 'Well, I've ruined everything, but it's out of my hands now. I'll have to let go and try to move on somehow.' I look down and take a deep breath; my lip quivers, but I manage not to cry. 'Maybe it's for the best anyway. I mean, Lexi and I couldn't live in the staff accommodation block with parties going on all night, and Lexi would have to change schools, and besides, there's no way I could leave my dog behind. I'll have to just get through the next couple of days and then we'll be going home anyway.'

Thalia cocks her head. 'I meant like… go and find Lexi and have some dinner…'

'Oh. Sorry.'

'I'm sure you'll work things out when you talk to him.' Thalia pats my arm. 'Why don't we go and get you ready for the ball? That will cheer you up.'

I stare at her blankly. 'I can't go to the ball! Not like this. Christmas is already ruined.'

'Cally,' Thalia says abruptly, 'you have to go – for Lexi.'

Her harsh tone makes my eyes fly open and knocks some sense into my thick head. Lexi. Lexi is all that matters.

'You're right, Thalia. Thank you. My crazy is showing, and I need to tuck it back in. My little girl needs a dress, and she needs her mum.'

'Why don't I go and find Lexi, and we'll meet you in the shop?'

'OK. Thank you. I don't want to ruin anyone else's Christmas by them seeing me in this state.'

Thalia zooms off, leaving me to nurse my second cocktail. I stir the straw around the ice cubes, my body slumped in resignation. I'm my own worst enemy. And now I have to suffer the consequences. He shouldn't have to step on eggshells to tell me he's living his dreams; it's no wonder he left.

But now what? He won't want to talk to me after the way I acted, and I don't blame him. I don't like myself much now either. So what do I do? Suffer the pain of holding out hope for the impossible? Or suffer the pain of letting go of everything I want? Or drag Lexi to Korea – a country I couldn't even point to on a map? My therapist has got one hell of a busy year coming.

I leave my half-empty glass on the table and make my way to the hotel shop, keeping my head down, trying to shut out *the most wonderful time of the year*. As far as

I'm concerned, *it's beginning to look a lot like shit-mas.* I can't even be bothered to shakira.

***

I no longer see the shop's magical twinkle when I step inside. This is merely a perfunctory visit for compulsory dress hire. And I definitely won't be wearing any silly shoes I can break my ankles in.

I skim over the rail of dresses, and in amongst all the icy-white gowns, I spot the one for me right at the back. Black. To match my mood. And my soul. And the empty space where my dreams once were. And, on a practical level, my pumps.

I pull out the dress and hold it up with a nod of approval. It's plain. No nonsense corsets or underskirts, just a functional dress that's long enough to cover my choice of shoes. Everyone else can wear these skimpy, glittering, white numbers. I already have a pallid, whiter-than-snow skin tone, and my inner beauty and sparkling personality shit will have to do. I nod and hmph. Like Miss Piggy. Ugh. That just about sums me up – I'm no Elsa.

I change into the black dress and come back out into the shop to check in the large golden mirror. At that moment, Lexi, Nanny P, and Thalia enter the shop.

Nanny P gasps, hand on her chest. 'You look beautiful,' she gushes. I shrug off her compliment, unable to appreciate it in my gloomy state. Thalia rushes over and, without a word, begins to pin the dress to make it fit and hang properly. 'I don't know if there will be time to sew it all, but these pins will hold everything in place. It will be fine, as long as no one touches you...' We both pause and consider her words. Thalia starts pinning again. 'Sorry, I didn't mean...'

'It's OK; no one will be touching me.'

I don't get time to wallow as Lexi then steps forward to offer her opinion. With her hands on her hips, Lexi shakes her head and simply says, 'No.'

'Why *no*, Lex?' I ask, amused by her candour. She almost makes her miserable mum laugh.

'Mum. It's Christmas. You look like a wicked witch or an evil queen. And *not* a beautiful Christmas princess.'

'Perfect! Just the look I was going for.'

Lexi is not amused. But this is the first time she's been inside the hotel shop, and she is immediately distracted by the sparkles. She gasps in delight at the sight of the dresses, her eyes lighting up with wonder. She starts to spin around, giggling with excitement as she takes in all the treasures on offer. And, taking after her mum, she wants to buy *everything*.

With her enthusiasm and cuteness, Lexi twists my arm into making this her first ever fantasy shopping spree. And not only does it provide a temporary cure for my misery, but it also gives me a new high.

When she twirls in her dazzling new gown, the look of pure ecstasy on Lexi's face lifts my spirits. Her glowing smile is priceless. If only the dress she chose was priceless too. But I shake away that thought, because my goodness, it's the dress of a young woman's fantasies – white and puffy, with brightly coloured ribbons tying the loose corset and streaks of colour beneath the sheer white overskirt, and... it lights up!

Soon, we cover the counter with our dresses and an array of sparkling accessories for Lexi – crystal-embellished shoes and shimmering jewels completing Lexi's fantasy ensemble. When it comes to paying, I brave a peep at the total price and wince, trying to hide my gasp from Lexi. Thank goodness for credit cards and that publishing advance. When I give the assistant my card, she pauses and checks some paperwork under the desk. She then taps some buttons on the till.

'Thank you, Ms Jackson.' She smiles and begins to wrap. 'Your items are complimentary, courtesy of the resort management.'

I almost faint, having to hold on to the counter to steady myself. 'Pardon?'

The assistant looks up and says, 'There's no payment due. We received a note from Mrs Todgers.'

'Oh, Diane,' I whisper.

***

After a mini-pampering, Nanny P takes a bouncing Lexi to the special children's Christmas Eve meal before the ball begins, leaving Thalia and I in my room.

'Ugh! I don't want to get ready. I don't know how I'm going to face this evening.' I fall back on my bed while Thalia sorts through my mish-mash of make-up.

'What's your plan, Cally?'

I know if she wasn't here with me, I would crawl into my bed and stay under the covers until morning. I take a deep breath. 'I guess I try to make myself invisible so I don't bump into him.'

'You don't want to try to talk things over?' she asks, frowning at my black pumps.

'He doesn't want to see me.' Groaning, I roll over, and while I'm yelling into my pillow, there's a tap on my leg. I turn back over to see a stern-looking Thalia standing over me with her hand on her hip. Lovely, sweet Thalia has been replaced by a *not putting up with my nonsense* Thalia, and she looks ready to whip me into shape.

'Up! You get in the shower, and I'll order some food.'

I drag my hand along the softness of the fluffy throw one more time as I stand up and give her a hug. 'Thank you.'

***

I'm trying to tame the frizz of my curls when there's a knock at the door, and Thalia walks over to let in room service. A smiling young man rolls in the trolley, the smell of pizza wafting around him, and I realise how hungry I am. There's also a bucket of champagne on ice with two glasses and a box. He wishes us a Merry Christmas and swiftly exits.

'I thought you could do with a drink too.' Thalia grins and opens the bottle. 'What's the box?'

'I was going to ask you the same thing.' I take a slice of pizza in one hand and lift the box lid with the other. We both peer inside and then look back at each other. I put the pizza back down and take a large glug of alcohol.

I take the short handwritten note from inside and read aloud, 'Cally, enjoy the ball. Jisung.'

I move the tissue paper aside and there are my beautiful, sparkling, impractical shoes with heels intact. 'He fixed them?' I stroke my finger along the crystals, then can't resist taking them out of the box and hugging them to my chest.

'He's still thinking of you,' Thalia says with her kind smile.

I look back at the note. 'But it just says *enjoy the ball*, not *see you at the ball*.' I pout, noticing there's no *love from*. Or *x*.

'You couldn't wear pumps with that dress anyway.'

I'm secretly pleased that I get to wear these beauties again too. I just won't do any running this time.

Thalia and I share the pizza and champagne, and then she helps with my make-up. Although I hadn't planned to wear any, with a stubborn attitude of *take me as I am, I have no one to impress*, I was overruled by Thalia's determination to help me feel confident in myself. And to be honest, Lexi's idea for Snow White–inspired blood-red lipstick looks pretty damn good. Though it's heartbreaking to realise it's my own fault that my lips won't be kissed by my handsome prince.

SATURDAY

Winter Ball

I don't know how I'm going to cope with seeing Jisung this evening. If he arrives with Abbi on his arm, I'll die on the spot. But there's no escape; it's time. I have to go to the ball.

Thalia takes my hand as she accompanies me down the grand staircase. 'Whatever happens, you will be OK,' she whispers. 'I'll be in reception if you need me.'

'Thanks again, Thalia. For everything. I don't think I would have got through this week without you.' We share a brief smile before I return my focus to not falling down the stairs.

The red carpet is laid at the bottom, ready to lead me through the Christmas tree path in the lobby and out of the main entrance.

'I won't have to put my boots on, will I?'

She giggles at me. 'No, the walkway is fully carpeted and covered.'

'Thank goodness. I think these pins would prick me to death if I had to bend over.'

'It's good to see you smile again.'

My heart rate speeds as we get to the bottom of the stairs, cameras clicking. 'I'm scared.'

'You are beautiful inside and out, Cally. Remember, what's meant to be will always find a way.'

'Thalia! There you are!' calls a member of the reception team.

'Oops, I better go. Have fun with Lexi.' She gives me a quick hug and a peck on the cheek before running back to her proper job. Leaving me alone. I'm frozen inside, but give forced smiles for the cameras as I head out of the doors.

Outside, the path is lined with glistening fairy-light-covered trees, the white floor strewn with pale-blue rose petals leading towards a huge marquee. The music and hubbub of guests get louder as I get closer, and I have to control my breathing so I don't panic myself into a heap.

As I stop outside the door, I discover a meaning of finding strength in solitude. It's me, standing here, trying to gather the confidence to go inside on my own, to move forward in my life, alone. If I have learned anything from Jisung, it's that I will be OK in the end. But how I wish I could skip straight to the scars and not have to cope with the open wounds.

Unfortunately, there's no basket full of strength with a sign saying *help yourself*. So I have no option but to do my best. And, failing that, fake it.

At the entranceway, I pause to soak in the enchanting atmosphere, mesmerised by the winter wonderland inside. From floor to ceiling, the marquee is decorated with floral displays dusted with snow and glittering diamond lights that look like falling snowflakes, all swathed in a soft blue glow. The beguiling ambience leaves me breathless, and I take a moment to ground myself.

I don't know how I'm going to find Lexi amongst all these people. Ah! Her dress! I'll look out for the lights.

I weave my way through the sea of whiteness – as I expected, most of the ballgowns are white, the decor is white, and many of the men are in white tuxedos. Wearing black means my plan to not stand out has failed. However, my functional dress is actually pretty awesome – off the shoulder, curve skimming, with a split to the top of my thigh that shows off my gorgeous shoes as I walk. It's even got hidden pockets. I can't help but walk tall and pout my kissy red lips. Even if I'm a total wreck inside.

I take a glass of champagne from a passing tray, pleased to have something to do with my hands, and stop to look at a large ice sculpture. Cinderella's glass slipper gleams on its platform. But I've gone right off fairy tales. Romantic nonsense that makes young girls grow up with ridiculous ideals and expectations that real life can never live up to. All she had to do was put on a shoe and then she lived happily ever after. Pah! It makes me more determined to write more books to show fairy tales for what they are – *lies*!

What if Rapunzel's mum was simply trying to protect her daughter from the cruel outside world? And what if dragons were peaceful, loving creatures who were hunted to extinction? Maybe a princess doesn't appreciate a stranger kissing her in her sleep? Or what if she was a sex-addicted vixen but the prince was more interested in the footman? OK, I'm not sure how suitable that would be for kids, but hmph. And yes, I am bitter. Why can't I have my Prince Charming and live happily ever after? I flounce away in a huff and continue looking for Lexi.

Eventually, I find her standing in front of an ornate mirror with Nanny P.

'Mum! You take a turn.' My little girl looks stunning, and the joy on her face warms my ice-sculptured heart.

'What is it, my darling?'

'Ask, *Mirror mirror on the wall, who's the fairest of them all?* It will answer.'

'Oh gosh, no! You're obviously the fairest of us all.' I don't need a stupid mirror to tell me there are others more fair than I. But Lexi's quite happy to accept my response. Stupid fairy tales.

A loud, merry commotion begins at the far end of the marquee, attracting everyone's attention with music and cheering and Ho! Ho! Hos! Lexi looks at me with her mouth open wide and then she's off. I follow at a more reasonable high-heeled pace along with Nanny P.

'How are you holding up?' she asks.

'I'm fine…'

She follows my gaze and pats my back. 'Ow!'

'Sorry, pins.'

Santa has arrived in a shiny red-and-gold sleigh pulled by four reindeer and accompanied by elves, with the star fairy-tale characters, including Prince Charming, as part of his entourage. I grab hold of Nanny P's arm for support, comfort, and any miracles she has going spare. She doesn't know the specifics of today's *Cally ruins her life* episode, but she can tell it's *something*.

'Deep breaths – you've got this,' she says.

Except I haven't got this at all. I can't take my eyes off him. His dazzling smile makes my knees weaken even while seeing him makes me want to cry. At least there's no sign of Abbi.

Children are laughing and squealing, catching presents and candies, and enjoying all manner of Christmas Eve fun that I want to escape from. I'm still holding on to Nanny P's arm, and she grips my hand in a way that says I am not alone. Or not allowed to run away. I keep my head down as the festivities go on around me. That is until the children take turns to sit with Santa in his sleigh to tell him their Christmas wishes – with their parents smiling happily next to them for photos.

Lexi has run to the front of the queue, and now there really is no escape from coming face to face with Jisung. And Santa, who left the condoms. Because this situation wasn't uncomfortable enough already. I finish my champagne in one glug and make my way forward without taking a breath.

Lexi sits next to Santa, with Jisung positioned behind her, facing me. I stand frozen, my pulse thundering in my ears. I can't bring myself to look up. The pain is unbearable, and I'm too old to cry in a photo with Santa. I fix my eyes on Lexi and fix a smile to my face. His intense stare penetrates my fragility.

Santa is a jolly old chap, chatting with Lexi and making her giggle. We pose for some photos, and then Santa says, 'So, Lexi, tell me. What is your Christmas wish?'

I listen eagerly, hoping that the computer game is still at the top of her list; otherwise there could be tears in the morning.

'I'm very sorry, Santa, but I've changed my mind since I sent you my letter.'

Oh no.

'My Christmas wish is to be here in Fairy-Tale Wonderland and live happily ever after in a family who all loves each other.'

I gasp, barely keeping my composure as my eyes fly up to meet Jisung's. My mummy heart breaks, and I choke back a flood of emotions. Jisung looks as shocked as I feel. My eyes still locked with his, I blink back tears of utter devastation until an elf cheerfully nudges me along for another family to take our place.

I drift back into the crowd to stand by Nanny P. She takes my hand and whispers, 'I'm sorry.'

Lexi is thankfully too excited by the special guest to notice her mum has crumpled behind her. Jisung continues to play his role, but in between children's turns, his eyes meet mine – although my eyes are too full of tears to read his expression.

It is soon time for Santa to wish us all a Merry Christmas and bid us farewell so he can take to the skies for his busy night. The children all wave goodbye, and guests make their way to the ballroom as the band begins to play. Nanny P is happy to take Lexi, and just as I see this as my opportunity to flee, Diane appears at my side.

Diane's wearing an elegant, understated golden gown, her warm and smiling face like a welcome ray of sunshine. I know she can see something's wrong but is too polite to ask questions right now. She, too, holds my hand as if a memo was sent out to all staff to ensure I don't disappear. I thank her for the generosity and kindness she showed Lexi and I with our dresses, always aware of Jisung in the corner of my eye.

We are both taken by surprise as a wave of noisy, festively adorned staff arrive in the marquee after clocking off work for the evening. It all feels a little chaotic, and I grip Diane's hand tighter, appreciative of the champagne we are offered.

Then my focus is solely on Jisung and the world stops spinning. Abbi is now draped over his shoulder, giggling, fondling the neck of his costume. Behind her stand tipsy-looking Georgia and Daisy. But Abbi looks quite drunk and on a flirtatious mission to capture *my* prince. Or is he *hers*? I guess this is when I get to see the truth.

He laughs along with the three of them. I could pass out any second as her hand glides under his jacket. She rubs his chest and begins to slide her fingers between his shirt buttons to touch his skin. I stumble backwards, catching Diane's arm to stop myself falling.

I'm not close enough to hear what Abbi's saying. But as I'm about to flee forever, I hear Jisung's firm voice: 'Please stop.' He lifts her hand and places it by her side, then steps aside to prevent her leaning on him. His head turns towards me, and his eyes lock onto mine. She stumbles forwards and reaches out for his body so she doesn't fall flat on her face. A face that now looks angry. He helps her stand, but his eyes don't stray from mine. I just stare; I am numb.

Abbi follows his eye line to me and growls, 'What's going on here?' Georgia grabs hold of her, restraining her from coming towards me. 'Am I missing something?' Her shouting makes me flinch, and I blink rapidly. Diane is right here. This can't be happening.

My eyes fly to Diane, who is watching the scene with tightly pursed lips and a very stern expression. Meanwhile, Abbi has pushed her way free of Georgia's grasp and is staggering towards me with a face of thunder. Although my heart is racing, I let go of Diane's arm and stand my ground.

Abbi stops in front of me and yells in my face, 'What's going on? Did you go after him behind my back?'

Georgia and Daisy try to pull her back, unsuccessfully. But they grab hold of her arms in case they swing for me.

'You went after my man?' she screams. But I stand firm.

Jisung then appears at her side and says quietly, but firmly, 'I have never been your man. Now step away from Cally and never speak to her like that again.'

'I'm fine, Jisung, but thank you,' I say quietly. I don't need him to save me this time.

Abbi turns to him with a scowl and shouts, 'Yeah, stay out of this! This has nothing to do with you!' She turns back to me, crosses her arms, and hisses, 'I thought we were friends. What happened to girl code?'

My stress levels have hit their peak, and where fight or flight has kicked in, my body's response is to fight back. On the outside, however, I remain as calm as I can. I can fall apart later.

'I don't have to explain myself to you, Abbi. But Jisung and I had something back in the summer – before you tried your luck.' Daisy and Georgia gasp. I daren't look to see Diane's reaction.

Abbi's eyebrows raise slightly, but she leans towards me and scoffs, 'Well, you can have that boring old man. I only went after him to get the points.'

Her laughter stops dead when Diane shouts, 'Enough!' Her arms chop through the space between me and Abbi. 'That is enough.'

Diane puts her hand on my arm. 'Cally, come away.'

As I take a step backwards, Abbi lurches towards Diane, her pointed finger just inches away from Diane's chest. 'You can't tell me what to do. I only answer to Frank.'

Diane remains stoic. 'Please leave before I have to call security.'

Jisung steps forward with his arm outstretched, ready to intervene, but Diane raises her hand for him to hold back.

Abbi places her hand on her hip and flicks back her hair. 'Frank would want to party with me.' Raising her chin, a sly smile smears across her face. 'I've got him wrapped around my little finger.' Diane doesn't move a muscle, despite having Abbi's little finger wiggling in her face.

Daisy pulls on Abbi's arm, but she holds still and her smile becomes a sneer. 'Just like I had my mouth wrapped around his... big finger, shall we say.' She turns to Daisy and Georgia with a chuckle and an obscene hand gesture. 'How many points do I get for that, hey?' They stare back, horrified, her vulgar implication hanging nauseously in the air.

The stunned silence is broken by Diane's calm voice. 'Yes, dear, and you'll have your final written warning and p45 waiting for you in the morning.'

Abbi jerks her head back around and screams, 'What? You can't sack me!

'I'm in charge now. I expect you off-site by midday. Merry Christmas, Abbi.'

Diane spins around and walks away with her head held high while Abbi screams after her, 'But it's Christmas! You can't sack me on Christmas Day!' Her friends finally manage to restrain her as she continues to rant her indignations.

I leave her to it and can't face Jisung right now. I immediately follow after Diane, in awe of how she just handled that situation. And sick to my stomach at what she's going to say to me.

Before I exit the marquee, I glance back. Jisung has gone. I manage to fall in step beside Diane, despite my shoes, and we march without a word to her office.

***

As soon as I close the office door behind me, she takes a bottle of brandy and two mugs from her desk drawer and pours two large measures. I just stand, waiting for whatever is to come next.

Diane sits, beckoning me over. I perch tensely on the couch as she passes a mug. We sip in silence, the brandy burning my throat.

'Diane, I'm so sorry.' I dip my head. 'I'm sorry you had to witness all of that. Please know I'm deeply ashamed, and I'm sorry you had to find out about me and Jisung this way, but most of all I'm sorry you had to hear that about Frank.'

She waves her hand and I look up. Somehow, she is giving me a small smile.

'How are you so calm?'

She sighs and slips off her shoes. 'Cally, he's been at it for years. It doesn't surprise me anymore, but I think I've had enough now.' She nods gently and takes another sip. 'I'll be shipping him off to Sunrise Valley as soon as they'll take him.'

'I... I don't know what to say...' I place my hand on her knee.

'Oh, don't worry about me. I'm fine, dear.' She smiles and pats my hand. 'Nothing gets past me. I hear everything that goes on around here. I do what I can to smooth things over after his mistakes. That will be one less job for me to do now.'

'I'm so sorry.'

We are quiet for a moment, although there's so much to process, so much to say. The brandy helps a little.

'My heart was broken a long time ago.' Diane looks down and swills her mug. 'Nothing could hurt me after the pain of losing Lottie.'

My heart breaks even more for her. But she sits up and brightens. 'I have a happy life here though. The staff are my family. I decided that was more important than romantic love.'

Diane starts to remove her jewellery. I'm still dreading her reaction to hearing about Jisung and I. She leans back and looks into my eyes. 'Cally, you are young. You have the chance of making a happy life here. I see that fire in your eyes.'

My stomach clenches and I twist towards her, staring as things click into place. 'Fire in my eyes? That was… you? My red dress?'

Diane nods with a sad smile.

'You were my fairy godmother,' I whisper under my breath.

She looks away. 'I'm sorry he was unprofessional and rude to you. I did what I could to make amends.'

'Oh my goodness, it's nothing for *you* to apologise for.' I reach over and give her a hug. 'And that's all in the past.'

Diane pulls back, her eyes fixed on mine with curiosity. 'Now, tell me what's happening with you and Jisung. Do you love him?'

'I… It… was beginning to seem that way.' My posture slumps as my thoughts turn back to my own situation. 'Are we in trouble?'

'Ha, no! He's gorgeous! I think we can make an exception to the rules for you. If I was thirty years younger, I'd be after him myself!'

We both snigger, and then my smile fades. 'But anyway, he's moving away, so that's it.' I sigh. 'The end of the line.'

'Moving away?' Diane sounds startled.

'He's going back to Korea to restart his acting career.' I down my drink, wishing it would numb the pain.

'Look, I probably shouldn't be the one to say, but Jisung is our new investor.'

My eyes flick up. 'Pardon?'

'It was his idea to build the family accommodation and start up our performing arts school. That's why he's had so many meetings recently. I don't think he has any intention of leaving for long.'

I jump to my feet and begin pacing back and forth. Diane pours more drinks.

'But then *I* went and ruined everything!' I cry, thoughts swirling over how I pushed Jisung away just as a future here was possible.

'How so?' Diane calmly passes my mug. I down the drink in one go – this news changes everything.

'I overreacted and gave him back his bracelet. He left me.' My face drops to my knees, making Diane stand and take me by the shoulders.

'Anyone can see how he feels about you. Abbi spotted it straight away.'

'So now what? What do I do?' I start pacing again.

'You need to decide what you want, dear. You might not have the luxury of time to think, *If it's meant to be, it will be*. My advice is, if you truly want him, go and get him.'

I stare back at her. I do know what I want. 'You mean like some grand gesture to try and win him back? But how? It's late Christmas Eve. There's no time to organise anything.'

'This is Fairy-Tale Wonderland.' Diane laughs. 'This is your fairy tale, Cally. Go and make your dreams come true.'

Just then, there is a knock at the door and Thalia bursts in.

'Sorry, Mrs Todgers. Cally, Lexi needs you. It's urgent.'

SATURDAY

Saranghae

I kick off my shoes and run out of Diane's office. 'Where is she? What's happened?'

'She's outside at the winter gazebo.' Even Thalia sounds flustered.

I run across to the cloakroom, get my boots, and slip my bare feet inside. I don't stop to tie my laces, just clomp out of the door.

'Good luck,' Thalia calls as I head outside.

What the hell has happened? Why isn't she at the ball? Panic rises through my chest. I should have been with her. And where's Nanny P?

I run towards the pool as best I can and call out Lexi's name. Silence. I'm not sure where this winter gazebo even is, but I spot a glow and head towards it.

I assume this is it – a white domed gazebo with a ton of white flowers and twinkling lights. But there's no one around, only bushes covered in snow.

'Lexi?'

I hear a faint muffled giggle and whirl around to where the sound came from. Just as I see the lights of her dress shining through the leaves, a hand touches my shoulder.

'Cally.'

I spin back to see Jisung. 'What's going on?' I grab on to his arms, my heart in my throat.

'Sorry,' he says gently. 'We didn't mean to scare you. I didn't know if you would come if I asked.'

Hand against my chest, I take a few deep breaths as relief begins to replace the panic.

'When did you plan this?' I ask, still recovering.

'Thanks, ladies,' Jisung says in the direction of the bush. 'Could you give us a few minutes?'

Nanny P's voice comes through the darkness. 'Of course. See you later.'

I watch Lexi's dress lights heading towards the hotel, then turn back to Jisung. My legs begin to quake, though I'm not sure if it's my bare skin in the cold air or nerves.

'Can we talk?' His voice is quiet, nervous.

'Sure,' I mumble into my chest.

Jisung and I stand under the beautiful, twinkling gazebo, with snowflakes beginning to fall like petals from the black winter's sky. It should be the most romantic night ever. But we stand in silence and I'm too ashamed, too scared, to look at him. Now the rush of adrenaline is wearing off, I start to shiver all over.

'Can I put my coat around you?'

I nod, and he unzips his coat, holding it open for me to walk closer. I gulp and step forward into the warmth of his chest. I close my eyes, trying to ignore my broken heart to soak up his closeness one last time. I rest my head against him and feel his chest rise and fall with short, quick breaths. He puts his coat around my body and pulls me closer.

'*Aish!*' he yells, making me jump and then giggle.

'Sorry, I have pins in my dress.'

He *carefully* pulls me closer to him and exhales in a sigh, which brings tears to my eyes. I was frightened, and I hurt him – and that pains me.

I wrap my arms around him beneath his coat and hold him tight. This is where I belong.

'I don't want to lose you.' The words burst from my mouth, and tears spill down my face. I grip him even tighter. 'I'm sorry I didn't listen and I overreacted again. I'm sorry I hurt you and made you walk away. And I'm sorry I'm making your shirt wet again.'

Jisung kisses the top of my head and reaches inside his coat for a handkerchief, then wipes my eyes.

'I'm sorry I wasn't more patient and that I left you alone. I never wanted to hurt you either.'

I finally look up to his face, breathing hard. 'And Korea?'

'I'll only be gone for six weeks. And then I'll be back… to stay.'

He cups my cheeks in his hands, his eyes glimmering with affection.

'Cally, you make me happier than I thought I could ever be. I know we haven't known each other long, but I know you are special – that what we have is special. I want to learn everything about you, inside and out.' He winks and I blush, giving a shy smile, as if he hasn't already seen all there is to see.

'So cute.' His flirty smile lingers. 'I want to support you to do all the things you want to do… And I want you to do the same for me. It might not always be easy, and we might have ups and downs – hopefully lots of those…' He smirks and wiggles his eyebrows at me, putting a big, silly grin on my face. 'I want us to share our burdens with each other. Let's have a fun adventure and see what we can become.'

My beautiful Prince Charming looks into my eyes, his face open and vulnerable, and my heart is ready to burst.

'What do you say, Cally?'

I put a hand to his face and slowly trace my fingers over his brow and back through his hair. I try to keep my voice steady. 'Jisung, you make me feel things I didn't believe in anymore, and I'm excited for a future I never thought was possible.'

My smile fades, and I look into his eyes. 'If I push you away, I need you to pull me back. And I'll try my best to be better, to be the best I can be for you, for us. I want to make you the happiest you've ever been.' We squeeze our bodies tightly together and I rest my forehead against him. Then, with a cheeky glint in my eyes, I tease, 'And you'll never want to dump me again.'

His eyebrows knit together. 'But… I never dum–'

'Just kiss me.'

He doesn't need to be told twice. He closes his eyes as he brings his lips down to meet mine, and he gives me a long, tender kiss that shows he means every single word.

When our lips part, Jisung dips his gaze. He pulls my bracelet from his pocket and dangles it between us. 'Can we share our dreams again?'

'Yes, please.' I'm filled with relief and happiness as he clasps the beautiful mushroom house back around my wrist. He kisses my hand and, without taking his eyes from mine, says in a louder voice, 'Lexi, you can come out now.'

I turn to follow the sound of giggles, and Lexi steps forward into the light. And if I'm not mistaken, the shadows behind her belong to a clapping huddle of Nanny P, Thalia, and Diane. I gesture for Lexi to join us, and she runs over. Jisung sweeps her up into his arms, and we all snuggle close together – for about a second, before Lexi wriggles free. Bubbling with excitement, she skips around me. 'Mum! Mum! Tell Prince Charming your poem.'

I put my hand on her shoulder to keep her still for a moment. 'What poem, Lex?'

'The one you wrote the other day. I found it on your bed.' She takes a scrap of paper out of her coat pocket and holds it up.

'I don't rememb– oh no…' I snatch the small piece of headed paper with the scrawl I wrote while half-asleep after my first night with Jisung. 'No, I can't, and I hope you didn't read it, Lexi.' I cover my face with my hand.

'You wrote me a poem? I'm touched.' Jisung's face lights up. 'Please read it. I've never had a poem written for me before.'

Ground please swallow me.

'Go on, Mum.'

'I'm so embarrassed. I apologise in advance.' I cringe and begin to read aloud – for Jisung's ears only…

'You are my sun that brings me hope,
With hugs that bring me joy.
My star that guides me through the dark,
And such a handsome boy!

'I want to hold your gentle heart,
Protect and love you so
You'll never doubt yourself again,
With this badass in tow.

'Our best moments are yet to come,
We'll laugh and play a while.

> *You'll always be my Charming Prince,*
> *I'll always make you smile.*
>
> *'Mid-night adventures we will find,*
> *Sunrises we will see.*
> *So long as we can both hold hands,*
> *And snog against a tree!'*

I keep my head low, expecting the sound of laughter. There is none, which can only mean he's cringing too, pitying my feeble, awful nonsense. Wincing, I raise my eyes. But he's smiling, fondly? He pulls me into a tight cuddle and whispers into my ear, 'That is the best gift I have ever received. Thank you.'

I'm in emotional overdrive, and I don't know what to say. My throat is tight, and I don't think I can speak without a deluge of tears. I respond with a kiss on his cheek just as Lexi stops jumping at our feet and tugs at Jisung's arm.

'Prince Charming...' She puts on her doe-eyed cutie-pie face. 'Please could you teach me how to speak in Korean?'

'Come.' He pulls Lexi into a family hug. 'The only word the three of us need to know for now is *Saranghae*.'

Lexi pouts, looking thoroughly disappointed. 'Does that mean *bedtime*?' Jisung laughs with such tenderness that I close my eyes to memorise the sound forever.

'It means *I love you*.' He smiles affectionately at Lexi and I, hugging us close. I melt into a soppy, lovey-dovey puddle. I think Lexi might have felt touched too, as she goes quiet for a short time before hopping away to waltz around the gazebo.

Chuckling, Jisung and I watch Lexi's theatrics as he pulls me close again. He smooths back my hair and kisses my forehead. 'Cally.' He looks deep into my eyes and takes a long breath, his hands tightening around me. 'Will you– wait! I forgot!' He breaks the spell of the moment as his body jerks stiffly upright and I pull back, my eyes pinging open wide. He scrabbles through his coat pockets until he produces a squashed sprig of mistletoe. Grabbing me back to his chest, a smile lighting up his face, he holds the mistletoe above our heads. 'Cally, will you be mine?'

'Kiss me again and I'm all yours,' I reply with the biggest smile. With this kiss, he shows me just how passionate he is. The mistletoe goes flying as he wraps his arms tightly around me. Beneath his cool, collected, charming persona, this man is all passion.

'Ewww! Gross!' Lexi intervenes, shaking her head, looking as though she's just tasted a Brussels sprout. 'Prince Charming, can I be a real princess now?'

Jisung swings her round in his arms. 'Yes, of course!'

My soul dances as I watch the two people I love laughing under the starry Christmas Eve skies in the heart of a glistening, snow-covered paradise.

Jisung puts my giggling little girl back on the ground and then gets down on one knee in front of us. My heart stops. He can't seriously be going to...

'Cally, Princess Lexi' – he smiles up at us both – 'would you do me the honour of spending Christmas day with me tomorrow? And perhaps, when the family accommodation is built, bring your dog and come and live with me here?'

Lexi runs in circles under the twinkling lights, leaping, and shouting, 'Yes!'

Jisung stands to face me and holds my hand to his heart. I'm speechless. My heart has turned to romantic mush. I nod, tears springing to my eyes. His gaze is intense and unyielding, and my heart flutters as he draws me close and presses a gentle kiss to my cheek.

This moment is pure magic, the kind that takes my breath away and leaves me feeling weightless with joy.

This is my fairy tale, right here. I've found my happily ever after.

Happily Ever After?

Dear Diary

Long time, no see! I came across you as I was sorting through my clutter and thought I'd give you a quick update. Gosh, how long has it been? Let's see. My last entry was just before we returned for our first Christmas at Fairy-Tale Wonderland – just over a year ago. The Christmas Jisung and I got together and the pieces of my broken life finally began to slot into place.

Jisung went to film in Korea in the new year, and although I missed him desperately, I was so busy that the time passed quickly. Lexi and I returned to Mother's, but thankfully only for the time it took to make arrangements to leave.

Somehow, amid the millions of forms I had to complete for Lexi to transfer schools, I worked my arse off.

My Winter Wonderland review was accepted by thirty-two publications… including (I'm still a little superstitious) the publication that shall not be named. Its global reach has more zeros than I can get my head around, and

I feel sick just thinking about the amount of ice cream Lexi and I ate to celebrate.

The influx of resort bookings earned me my first ever bonus! And get this... I treated myself to a brand-new handbag!!!

Lexi and I were back where we belong in time for spring term at her new school. The street cred for living at an exclusive holiday resort meant she was immediately invited to join the group of cool kids. Thankfully they weren't mean girls and were actually quite sweet. I was even invited to meet some of their mothers at a Ladies Lunch. Two of them have since become new friends!

But I digress. Where were we? Oh yeah, moving in. While the family accommodation was being built, Lexi and I had our own room in the hotel. Spoilt or what?! Out of school hours, Lex gets to join in the kids' club activities, and she's still best friends with Nanny P and Baby Bear. She couldn't be happier.

Diane has become a firm friend, as have Thalia, Daisy, and Nanny P (I can't get used to calling her Prim). Thalia was promoted, as per my suggestion, and Frank was indeed shipped off to be cared for at Sunrise Valley, so Diane is far less stressed. Daisy found a new love in Tom, the barman from the small hotel bar, and they are so cute together. Georgia was promoted after Abbi left, so she's doing well too. And I have a little group of friends who I adore, and they have become like family.

I have the best work environment, with unlimited sources of inspiration and places to think and write. But the couch by the round window is my favourite. And I have been a busy bee, creating stories about each of the resort's characters, as well as writing my alternative fairy tales.

The publishing process is unbelievably long; the Cinderella book is currently being illustrated, so none of the series has yet been printed. But plans are underway for a big launch party later this year, hosted, of course, by Fairy-Tale Wonderland. Which will lead to writing another article advertising the resort as an exceptional events venue.

My divorce eventually came through, but I don't want to waste any further ink on the matter.

Especially when I can move on to my favourite topic… Jisung.

Talk about a whirlwind – where do I even start? I still get butterflies every time I see him, and his smile still makes me giddy, and my insides are still soppy mush. He is the love of my life, my dream come true. And although I feel shy writing the words, I am his too. We make each other happier than we ever could have imagined.

It's been hard not living together – I never want to let him go, although our goodnight kisses are breathtaking. And we're still working on balancing our busy work schedules with family life.

As the resort's new investor, Jisung became a director alongside Diane, and to make time to manage all his different projects, he decided to recruit and train a new Prince Charming.

Enzo's character persona sends the women wild, but underneath he's a sweet mama's boy who misses home. We've adopted him as our little brother, and he's great fun to have around. He's brought us hours of entertainment with his efforts to woo Thalia.

But Jisung will always be my Prince Charming. He's been starting up the new stage school, which Lexi has joined and is loving every minute of. And I've been encouraging him to pursue his acting and supporting him every step of the way. I learned my lesson.

He went back to film another series in Korea in the autumn, and he loves being able to come home here to avoid all the paparazzi nonsense. The media have enjoyed the mystique and have left his family, and us, in peace.

We take it in turns to arrange our dates – usually something simple, a picnic or a walk with Barney, watching how the beautiful landscape changes with the seasons. It's much easier now we don't have to hide that we're together. Regrets over past misunderstandings have long faded, and our time alone is always magical.

Jisung's been learning that I can't drop everything at a moment's notice when he has free time. And I've been learning that it's safe to trust him, that he's not going to run off, that I'll never find another woman in my house.

Talking of houses, our family is finally about to be united. As we pack for our new apartment, I can picture the lazy mornings together and family dinners. I can already feel the warmth of our new home, and I can't wait for Barney dog to join us too. He's been staying with Diane and is one pampered little pooch!

Lexi is over the moon to get her own bedroom. And at long last, Jisung and I will have our own room with our own bed and our own private space. No more sneaking around, finding discreet locations! (Although I suspect we may continue with that too.)

Anyway, back to the Christmas just gone. We celebrated our first year together with another illicit evening in Santa's cabin, packed with incredible knee-trembling, earth-moving treats. However... this time, Santa didn't leave us any condoms...

So while I was expecting the imminent arrival of my menopause, I am now expecting the arrival of something I definitely hadn't anticipated.

I am now what has been referred to as a 'geriatric' mother-to-be. Talk about rubbing it in.

And while I am able to almost calmly write these words, trust me, I was not in any way calm when I discovered the gift Jisung had given me that night.

Nappies and no sleep. At my age.

I took Jisung trekking one evening, up the hill and all those steps to watch the fireworks. I waited for the shooting-star firework at the end. He held me in his arms, his gaze meeting mine, as he wished for the three of us – Lexi, me, and him – to be happy and healthy. In that tender embrace, I softly kissed him, sharing the same heartfelt wish for the newest addition to our perfect little family.

He took a long moment. I thought he would be pleased when I told him. I wasn't expecting him to leap off the ground and punch the air, shouting, 'Yes! My sperm is awesome!'

I also wasn't expecting him to then get down on one knee, take off his ring – the precious ring that belonged to his mother – and ask me to marry him. When I managed to say yes through my blubbing, he placed it on my finger, shedding a few tears himself. We didn't notice the lanterns floating by that night. After all, I no longer had to keep my hands to myself.

The wedding of my, I mean, *our* dreams is planned for June. It's going to take place under the domed gazebo with its cascade of flowers and twinkling lights. I shall have a gorgeous, probably giggling bridesmaid by my side, and a groom too amazing for words.

The events team is organising the whole thing with the help of my vivid imagination and Fairy-Tale Wonderland's incredibly generous budget. It's going to be the most magical day ever.

And we've been looking at a family honeymoon in Korea.

Obviously, an article will follow advertising Fairy-Tale Wonderland as an exquisite new wedding venue. Maybe I'll even write a new book about how a bog witch became a princess.

So nappies and no sleep? Yes. And first smiles, first words, first steps… A loving family living in paradise with a devoted dad and the proudest big sister.

When I think of the love and joy and meaning Lexi has brought into my life, it's hard to imagine how my heart could possibly expand to experience that again. But now, as I feel my little bump growing and flourishing, I am already overwhelmed with love.

Jisung dotes on me and my belly and won't let me lift a finger. I've never felt so cherished and cared for, and my heart is bursting with happiness for this beautiful, growing family of mine.

See? I'm a hormonal, soppy mess, bordering on adding a #blessed.

Seriously though, I thank my lucky stars every single day for the blessings that fill our lives.

You know, dear diary, I used to think that fairy tales were only for children and that happy endings were just a myth. But now, geriatric or not, I know for certain that we are never too old for fairy tales; we never know what could be just around the corner to make our dreams come true.

It took me a while to get here, and there were times when I felt like giving up, like I was never going to find my way. But looking back at all the ups and downs of my journey, I realise that every step was worth it. Every challenge, every setback, every triumph... they all led me to this moment, this feeling of pure bliss.

My heart is overflowing with gratitude, like a garden bursting with life. Every day brings new blossoms and new joys and new dreams. Dreams that are alive and continue to grow and change as time progresses.

Our happily ever after is not the end of our story; it is the beginning of a new adventure, a new chapter in our fairy tale. And I can't wait to see what the universe has in store for us as life goes on.

Dear Wonderful Reader

Thank you for joining me in this winter wonderland adventure of Happily Ever After? I hope it has warmed your heart and filled you with Christmas magic!

I have loved writing about Cally's journey to find happiness and I shall miss her now it's all over. If only Fairy Tale Wonderland was a real holiday resort... (Sigh) Not that I could ever afford to go... (Big sigh) And if only dreamy Prince Charming was a real person... (Swoon) (Please don't tell my husband I said that!)

Thank you once again for your support and for allowing me to share my story with you. I would love to hear what you liked about this sequel, and would be very grateful if you could leave a quick review on Amazon or Goodreads. Your kind words will help other readers journey to Fairy Tale Wonderland too!

Warmest regards
Melissa

Acknowledgements

At the heart of every book lies a supportive community working behind the scenes. My journey wouldn't have been possible without the incredible individuals who have stood by me, and for that, I am sincerely thankful.

With special thanks to:
Amy, Annie, Dana, Ellie, Jackie, Jennifer, Laura, Marie, Mumma, Rachel, and Yvonne.

Chloe Cran, my incredible editor, who made this all possible.

My awesome ARC Team, my wonderful family, and of course, BTS and fellow ARMY.

Author Bio

I'm Melissa John, a British writer and 40-something mum, inspired by my obsessive fangirling over Kpop and KDrama, and with a passion for escaping into enchanting worlds of whimsy and romance. I love to write heart-warming stories for women in midlife who follow their dreams to create their own happy endings.

Email
melissa@melissajohn.co.uk
Facebook
melissajohnauthor
Instagram
@melissajohnauthor

Reader Bonus

Delve into the visual world of *Happily Ever After?* through this curated Pinterest board. Lose yourself in the enchanting imagery that accompanies each chapter and let your imagination soar.

Pinterest
bit.ly/PinHEA

Printed in Great Britain
by Amazon